Flying to the Light

Elyse Salpeter

Flying to the Light

Copyright © 2011 by Elyse Salpeter

Cover Artist – LLPix Photography

This book is a work of fiction. The names, characters, places, and incidents are products of the writer's imagination or have been used fictitiously and are not to be construed as real. Any resemblance to persons, living or dead, actual events, locale or organizations is entirely coincidental. The author/and publisher does not have any control over and does not assume any responsibility for author or third-party Web sites or their content.

Published in the United States of America

First print edition: September 2011 Cool Well Press, Inc.

Second Edition: KeBen Press March, 2014

Dedication

This book is dedicated to the people in my life who have been my support system. My RWs, a group of the most talented authors I know, have been my writing lifeline, letting me throw out any crazy idea I've had. They've read my work, critiqued, edited, and been my greatest friends and teachers in the writing world. Denise Vitola, Mitchel Whitington, Bob Nailor and David Hilton, a huge thank you.

I want to thank Beth Ryden for believing in me and giving me my very first opportunity to jump into the publishing world. I will be forever grateful to her.

I also want to thank my husband, Steven, an avid reader who has strayed far from his comfort world of non-fiction to read my fiction books and short stories. For taking the kids out when I've needed time to write, for making the dinners when I've had a deadline, and for being a great supporter.

Lastly, I want to thank my children, Ben and Kelly, for giving their mommy the time to immerse herself in her fantasy worlds when they'd rather I was outside playing on the swing-set, playing board games, or looking for bugs under rocks. They have been my inspiration and I hope to make them proud.

Flying to the Light

Prologue

My arms heaved with effort as I pushed Danny higher on the swing. His shrieks of delight egged me on until he was so high he seemed to be soaring to the sky. My mother would have killed me had she seen this.

A clicking noise caused me to turn my head, and I saw a man taking pictures. I could have sworn he was taking them of Danny and me. I turned to him, ignoring Danny's complaints that I had stopped pushing.

The man lowered the lens from in front of his eyes and smiled. "You've got a cute brother there."

"Thanks," I mumbled.

The man turned and started taking photos of the park, concentrating on a flock of sparrows pecking at flecks of food on the ground near our swing set.

The man glanced up at me again, grinning. "Big birdwatcher."

That smile gave me the creeps. What a weirdo.

Danny jumped off the swing mid-flight and landed in the sand. I took his hand and pulled him to another part of the park, away from the photographer and his camera. I could hear the clicking of the shutter as we walked away, and I tried hard not to imagine he was really taking photos of us and not the birds.

Chapter One

Day 4—Thursday, 5:00 a.m.

He felt old. Not the kind of old where someone simpers along in a blessed Alzheimer's oblivion and nurses tend to your every need, but the kind of old that nightmares bring. The old that if he closed his eyes to go to bed for the night, there would be the lingering fear he might not wake up in the morning—that this might be his last cognizant night on Earth.

Michael was so terrified he couldn't breathe. His safe, little world had shifted out of its comfortable orbit the moment his parents were kidnapped, propelling him to places he never dreamed imaginable. Suddenly, there was horror everywhere and nothing was what it appeared to be. How could life go so terribly wrong in just a few hours? He had had no time to think. He couldn't plan, but just reacted to what was happening. A storm, more volatile and dangerous than a level five tornado had turned his world inside out and all he could do was attack it head-on, swallowing his fear and living strictly on the adrenaline pumping furiously throughout his body, hoping against hope his luck wouldn't run out.

The only thing he knew was that now his little brother was his responsibility. An innocent six-year old who for some reason the world wanted to claim as its own to exploit.

Michael wouldn't let them win. He would protect his brother with his life.

He glanced at Danny, who had fallen asleep in the passenger seat. He could see his brother's furrowed brow and pale face in the flickering glow of the highway lamplights. Michael felt like they'd been through a war, racing right along with the military guys in the Middle East right now.

Just as the rain began hitting the windshield, Danny started to whimper.

"Don't worry. I won't let anything happen to you." He wondered if he could fulfill that simple promise. He took one hand off the wheel and patted his brother's head. Danny immediately calmed. Still, he wouldn't have responded even if Michael had shouted. Danny was deaf, and that, among other things, was one of the reasons they were in this car fleeing across the country. They were running far away from their home, trying desperately to get to a small town in northern California. Mr. Daley had said there was a man there who could help them. Daley was Michael's high school biology teacher and the only person in Rockland County who wasn't out for the glory, the money, the prize of scientific discovery, or the chance to see the light.

The Night Before

Day 3 Wednesday 9:30 p.m.

"Michael, what the hell are you doing here?" Daley asked, incredulous when he and Danny, having nowhere else to turn, stormed into the biology classroom. The teacher had been working late, setting up science experiments for the next day's lessons, and was just in the middle of laying out rows of beakers when they burst in on him. One look outside at the advancing mob, brandishing their sticks and bats, and he knew what was happening. How could he not? He had seen the boys' faces plastered all over the evening news. The things they had been accused of. He immediately ran over and shut off the overhead lights so as not to attract the attention of the mob. Turning on the small lamp next to his desk, he turned to the boys, and didn't like what he saw.

The Michael before him was not the young man who had been in his class days before. The calm and humble introvert who preferred to hide behind his long dark hair rather than admit to anyone how brilliant he really was had disappeared. Now he was nearly unrecognizable from his former self. Deathly pale and sweating profusely, he ran his hands through his hair and paced the room, racing from one window and then back to the door to make sure it was locked, and then repeating the actions, over and over. He reminded Daley of a drug addict in need of a fix. Danny was no better. His dark brown eyes were wide, fearful saucers as he watched his brother do his strange dance, a look of helplessness spread across his features and showing in his sunken sockets.

He heard fighting outside. There wasn't a lot of time. Daley grabbed the pad on his desk and started scribbling. "We've got to get you guys out of here before that mob finds you. This is the name and address of an old friend of mine. He'll be able to help you. At the very least, it'll put some distance between you and them." He jerked his head towards the window.

Michael glanced out the window again. "Who is he? Another teacher? Someone from the government?"

Michael's voice rose agitatedly, bordering on panic, and Daley knew he had to calm him down, had to get him under control. "He's someone you can trust. He'll know what to do. Here, I'm giving you my car." He handed Michael the keys, but the kid started to protest. After running with his brother for days, the boy must be exhausted and probably felt he couldn't trust anyone. Well, his feelings didn't matter right now. Michael had to listen to him. It was the only way to keep him safe.

Daley grabbed the kid's elbows and pulled him close until their faces were only inches apart, forcing Michael to confront him.

Michael tried to pull away, started to fight him, but Daley held him firm. "Get it together, kid. You're not a child, so don't act like one."

Michael stared defiantly at his teacher, his green eyes squinting angrily. It was a look Daley was relieved to see. The kid hadn't lost it completely.

"Good," he started. "Your brother needs you and you're the only person who can help him right now. Do you understand me?" He forced the keys and note into Michael's hands, squeezing the kid's fingers closed around them.

Michael didn't say anything, but he took them and Daley breathed a sigh of relief.

Daley felt Danny by his side. He looked down, and the little guy took his palm and kissed it. A moment later five black crows landed on the windowsill, squawking loudly.

Daley stared at the birds, trembling. It's true, he thought, awed. He pulled his gaze away from the window and spoke quickly. "It's time to go. The car is in the back parking lot, the blue Honda with a Badgers Football bumper sticker. And here, take this, too. You'll need it." He opened his wallet and took out some cash. He placed it in an envelope, which had been on his desk and thrust it into Michael's hands. Daley then ushered them down the back staircase and out the rear entrance of the school towards the parking lot.

As the boys pulled out of sight, the tires squealing against the pavement, the first group of townspeople began searching the school. He heard their muffled shouts echoing through the empty halls. Daley breathed a sigh of relief until the crowd noticed the small flock of birds on the sill and went into a frenzy. Immediately, they started breaking doors and smashing windows, all trying to be first to get into the school and apprehend Danny.

Hidden in the shadows, Daley took out his cell phone and dialed. When the familiar voice answered, he smiled. "They came just like I told you they would. I sent them on a wild goose chase to some phony address in California near the home base. No, Mr. Herrington, don't worry about it, the car's got a tracking device. We'll pick them up once they get out of state. Have your men keep close tabs on them until I call in next." He closed the phone and put it back in his pocket.

Daley turned to stare at the school, shaking his head. A window in his lab shattered as someone threw a chair out of it.

"Run, my boys, run," he whispered to himself, turning and disappearing into the night.

Michael glanced up from the road for a moment and using his thumbnail, he opened the envelope Daley had given him. Inside was four hundred dollars. His anger at his teacher for treating him like a child abated and he calmed down, shaking his head at the generosity the man had shown. His turned his gaze to Danny. He was sound asleep, but Michael knew he was probably dreaming of birds, and, of course, the light.

Chapter Two

Two Days Earlier

Day 1, Monday 4:30 p.m.

"Gary, did you see my bracelet?" Maddy searched the top of her night stand and opened her jewelry box for the second time. Earrings and necklaces were strewn across her dressing table.

"I think you were wearing it when we were wrestling last night." He walked by and smacked her lightly on her backside with his towel.

She whacked him on his arm, but was charmed. After almost twenty years of marriage she was still madly in love with this man. He wasn't your typical middle-aged man with a beer paunch the size of a seven-month pregnant woman and so out of shape he couldn't run up the steps without having a coronary. He seemed younger than his years with his full head of hair, just starting to show the tell-tale signs of age with those cute grey strands at his temples.

She turned back to her jewelry box, grabbed a pair of earrings and made her way into the living room. She passed Michael, who swigged milk out of the carton from the refrigerator and rolled her eyes at him. "Must you do that? You're going to give your brother terrible ideas."

"I know, the little copycat." He wiped the milk mustache on his sleeve and then laughed at his mother's disgusted expression.

Maddy shook her head in defeat and continued into the living room. She didn't really mind this idiosyncrasy in her eldest son, albeit a disgusting one. The kid was every mother's dream. He was smart, funny, a great brother to Danny, and if he wanted to ruin every sleeve on all his shirts, so be it.

As she searched underneath the couch cushions, Michael strolled into the room, passing Danny as he watched a cartoon on the television. "What are you looking for anyway, Mom?"

"My bracelet. You know, the one Daddy got me for my birthday last year with the rubies and emeralds on it."

"You mean the one Mr. Teddy's wearing?"

Maddy glanced up and stared at Danny. There in his lap was his stuffed teddy bear from Build-A-Bear wearing a baseball uniform and a beautiful 18K gold-link gem bracelet.

Maddy walked in front of the TV to get Danny's attention, and started signing. "Do you think Mr. Teddy would mind if I had my bracelet back?"

Danny giggled and signed back. "Mommy, Mr. Teddy likes your bracelet."

"I'm sure he does, but he doesn't have to go out to an awards dinner this evening with a group of boring research scientists and I do. Let's go, little man. Hand it over."

Danny sighed, gently removed the chain from Mr. Teddy, and delicately gave it over to his mom.

"So, Mr. Teddy likes jewelry now, does he?" Michael signed to Danny, teasing him.

"The bracelet was a present from the birds," Danny answered.

Michael grabbed a throw pillow from the couch and threw it at his brother. "Everything with you is a present from the birds. You know what? I'm going to start calling you Birdman."

Danny giggled and threw back the pillow. It fell short of Michael's feet.

"Okay, guys, enough." Maddy turned to face them. "So, how do I look?"

"Seriously, you look great, Mom," Michael signed.

Danny nodded, signing, too. "You look beautiful."

"Thanks, boys." Maddy stared at her sons, feeling a love so intense she couldn't breathe for a moment. She was incredibly fortunate. Almost seven years ago, when she had learned that her stomach aches weren't the flu, but a pregnancy, she and Gary had been gloriously happy. For years they had tried unsuccessfully to have another child and had practically given up, but surprises sometimes just happened.

Both Maddy and Gary were successful research scientists working for Hi-Core Industries, an American bio-engineering firm which conducted a wide range of experiments for the United States Government. Everything from pharmaceuticals to genomes was being worked on by scientists from all over the country. The Anderson's specialty was an up-and-coming area in neuroscience on light therapy for seniors. The use of light therapy to stop depression was already being conducted on patients, but Maddy and Gary's project utilized light therapy for curing a multitude of brain related issue functions in everything from Alzheimer's to Parkinson's disease.

For their efforts, they were both receiving an award from the Scientific World Council. The award only went to one research group per year and entrants from all over the globe were considered. It was a great honor, and Gary and Maddy were ecstatic to have their work finally recognized on an international level. This award would offer them the opportunity to receive the attention they needed to gain more access to research documentation at facilities around the world, not to mention grants to keep the project going. There was still so much work to do, and she had her eye on a Nobel Prize down the road.

Gary strolled into the room, putting on his tuxedo jacket. "The woman you see before you boys is the new Queen of

Light Technology." He pointed at Michael and winked. "If you play your cards right, kid, you too can marry the computer geek of your dreams."

Maddy giggled and turned, fixing his bow tie. "Let's go, Romeo." She turned to Danny. "Okay now, I want you to be good for your brother. You got that?"

Danny nodded.

She turned to Michael and spoke aloud. "Do me a favor. Try to keep him out of the backyard. For some reason, we keep finding dead birds out there. I think they're eating the wild berries from the bushes in the woods, which makes them all drugged, and then they fly right into the house. The ones in the back are burned, like they've been baking in the sun all day. We'll figure out what to do with them tomorrow. Oh, and if you need to reach us, we'll be at the Plaza Hotel in New York City. The phone number is on the counter. I'll have my cell phone with me, too, honey, but you know how sketchy it is. I don't always get reception on the darn thing. Expect us back around two o'clock in the morning, though I hope you'll be sleeping by then. We'll be attending the awards party after the event until about one o'clock and then we'll come straight home. There shouldn't be any traffic at that time." She gave him a kiss on his cheek, brushing his hair back from his face. "And remind me to get you a haircut tomorrow."

His dad walked over. "Michael, don't forget to finish your term paper on the condor."

"Okay," Michael said.

Gary raised his eyebrows questioningly. "Really? Just get it done. 'Night boys." He took Maddy's arm and swept her out of the house.

No sooner had the door shut when Maddy popped her head in again. She ushered Michael towards her. "Michael, do me a favor. Keep Danny away from the windows and all those dead birds. I don't want him to get scared, okay?"

"Sure, mom. Don't worry, we'll be cool. Have a great time tonight."

"I love you, baby," she said.

With that, the door closed, and the boys were on their own.

Chapter Three

Michael finally coaxed Danny into bed at nine o'clock and then kicked back to watch TV, a can of Coke, and a bag of barbecue potato chips resting on his stomach. His term paper on the condor sat unfinished, open on the laptop next to him.

He was just dozing off when a segment on the eleven o'clock news about a murderous rampage at the Plaza in New York City caught his attention. He was almost immune to reports of shooting sprees by maniacs since they were plastered across the news all the time, but this one piqued his interest. Michael sat upright with a start, the empty bag of chips falling forgotten on the floor.

Five assassins had swarmed into an awards presentation at the Plaza at ten-thirty that evening and started a shooting spree, which left five people dead and at least fifteen injured.

Survivors said after only a few minutes of searching the crowd, men grabbed a couple and dragged them from the room and out through the kitchen. So far the suspects hadn't been apprehended, and the FBI was scouring the hotel for leads. Michael listened, sweating and nauseous, as the newscaster announced they would report more details as soon as they came in.

Michael rushed to the phone and called the number his mother had given him at the Plaza in case of emergencies. All the lines were jammed, and he couldn't get through. He punched in the numbers to her cell phone, but it went right to voicemail. "Mom, Mom, please call me when you get this," he shouted into the phone.

He couldn't believe this was happening. He pictured his mother and father leaving that evening, never for one moment thinking anything would possibly happen to them.

Michael ran back into the living room to watch the news, hoping the deep, sinking feeling in his stomach was just nerves and not a horrible premonition. He kept glancing at the door, desperately wishing his parents would burst in and tell him they were fine and he shouldn't have worried. He turned back to the newscast, tears streaming unnoticed down his face.

Michael's parents didn't come home that evening and after a sleepless night, the eight a.m. news made him sick to his stomach, his worst fears confirmed.

A grim-faced announcer filled the screen. "The hostage victims have been identified as Madeline and Gary Anderson, two of the neurophysicists being presented with awards last evening. The police have uncovered evidence believed to be left behind by the kidnappers, though at the present time they are unclear as to its meaning. The kidnappers dropped a bag in the hotel kitchen filled with snapshots of birds and photos of a little boy who has just recently been identified as Daniel Anderson, the six-year-old son of the Andersons. What they are most interested in is a set of notes allegedly linking the kidnapped victims to Samuel Herrington's organization. He is being contacted as we speak."

Samuel Herrington? The crazy corrupt biophysicist who once tried to buy his way into NATO? Michael remembered reading about this guy a few years ago. How Herrington thought he could intimidate everyone with his billions and his secret laboratories where he claimed he had at his disposal enough bio-chemicals to bring down the entire human race. Reports of his doings created panic around the globe, but the FBI and Homeland Security assured everyone none of it was true and Herrington was no threat to anyone. That the government had gained access to his labs and there were no bio-agents of that magnitude at any of his facilities.

Still, there was always talk when unexplained atrocities occurred around the globe. Was Herrington responsible for the recent strain of a virulent flu, which left thousands of people dead across Europe? Or was he the one responsible for the thousands of dead fish that washed up on the shores of the Philippines last month? What about the disappearing Coral Reef?

Herrington claimed he was a philanthropist, dedicated to finding cures for diseases, such as cancer and diabetes and constantly pushed his agendas in Africa, where he offered free vaccinations to thousands of people to help fight everything from malaria to whooping cough.

But other people weren't so sure, including Michael's parents who were constantly glued to the news when anything related to this guy came on. They were more concerned with his side interests. The stuff most people ignored, like Herrington's weird curiosity about death, or his obsession with numbers and colors.

Michael was fascinated with government conspiracies and read alternative collusion websites. So many rational people thought the government was covering up things for their own agenda. That they may even be conspiring with Herrington on some level. The mere mention of the man's name gave Michael the shivers, and the thought of his parents being linked to Herrington scared him to death. The guy had power, money and frankly, seemed a little skeevy whenever he saw him on television. It wasn't so much what he looked like, but how he moved. He was nearly always dressed in a perfectly pressed gray striped suit, when he wasn't in his tennis whites. Whenever he was on the news, he would pat his head, as if his gray hair wasn't slicked back enough from his forehead. And for a guy, he wore an awful lot of jewelry. Jeweled rings on many of his fingers, diamond tie clips, a watch that sparkled so much the lights from the cameras would glare off of it, as if Herrington had to continuously boast to everyone how rich he was. The problem Michael had with him was how his eyes would constantly shift around as if he were expecting someone to come at him suddenly. How he would never shake anyone's hand. The way he spoke, like a robot, so cold and monotonous, as if he were giving a lecture all the time, rather than just having a conversation with regular people. Michael didn't trust anything the guy said.

He lowered the sound on the TV and heard a car door close outside the house. Inching quietly to the window, he peeked through the living room curtains and saw an unmarked brown sedan idling across the street from the house. Two uniformed officers stood outside the car, talking and staring at the house.

Excited, he ran to the door and was about to open it when the phone rang. He picked it up, hoping it was his parents.

It wasn't.

"Michael?" The voice was familiar.

"Dobber?" Michael asked. "Is that you?"

Dobber was Dennis Dobbernesky, one of the scientists who worked at his parent's lab. He was a funny, gentle guy, always telling jokes, doing science experiments like oozing liquid or blowing things up to make them laugh when they visited.

He wasn't laughing now. "Michael, where's Danny?"

"He's still sleeping. Dobber, did you hear what happened to my parents?"

Dobber ignored him. "Listen to me. You have to get Danny and you as far away from those cops at your house as possible. Do you hear me? They're not real policemen. They work for Samuel Herrington. The people who took your parents are now coming to get you."

Michael's head was spinning. "What are you talking about? Why would they come to get us? And how do you even know the police are here?"

Dobber raised his voice, seething with frustration. "I can't explain it to you now. There are things you don't know, things which were kept from you to protect you. You have to trust me. Get out of the house right now and run. These people want Danny."

"Why would they want my brother?"

A knock sounded on the door.

Dobber started yelling at him. "Run now, don't let them in, please. Danny has to be protected. His powers are growing and these monsters are going to use him unless you protect him. Don't trust anyone, Michael."

Suddenly the line went dead. As Michael stared at the phone in shock, the knock sounded again. He turned to the door, unsure. Dobber was one of the nicest, funniest and most laid back guys he had ever met. He never raised his voice. Why would he be scared of the police? This had to be a mistake.

Michael put down the receiver and walked over to the door. He opened it a crack, staring at two smiling police officers.

A female cop stepped forward. "Hi, Michael, are you boys okay? Our lieutenant had us come over to check on you after we realized what happened to your parents. I'm sure you're scared." She flashed her badge and credentials at him.

She looked so kind, so…normal. He nodded. "I am."

"Do you mind if we come in? We've been told to escort you both to the police station to protect you and see if maybe you can tell us a little bit more about your parents so we can try to help them." She smiled and leaned in, touching his arm. He opened the door further, her smile widening. "Don't worry. We'll find your parents. I'm sure they're okay or we would have heard something by now."

Her voice was calming. Michael turned to the other cop, a guy, who nodded reassuringly. He could feel himself being swayed. Without thinking, he opened the door the entire way. The police officers came in and stood in the living room.

"Let me go get my brother, okay?"

"Sure." They nodded. "Want some help?"

"No, let me just wake him up and get a few things together for him." As Michael moved down the hallway he saw the woman pick up a photograph of his family and show it to the male cop. He nodded, and she put it down.

Michael went into his room and threw some of his clothes into a backpack and then, suddenly overwhelmed, he sat hard on the edge of his bed and put his face in his hands. Images of his parents being hurtled through the hotel at gunpoint and being tortured raced through his head. He wanted to scream in helplessness and started to cry. He prided himself on becoming a grown-up, but he felt more like a child than ever.

His dad's voice echoed through his head. Think of Danny.

That made Michael sit up straight, and he wiped savagely at his eyes. The police were here and they could help. Dobber had made a mistake. How did he even know the cops were here? That thought niggled at the back of his mind as he grabbed a few more personal belongings, went into Danny's room, and gently woke him. "Get dressed, Danny, we're going on an adventure."

"Can Mr. Teddy come, too?" he signed, yawning.

Michael wasn't sure if he would laugh or cry. In a six-year-old's mind, a teddy bear could offer all the comfort you ever needed in the world. He wished he had his own magical bear to make this go away. "Sure, just hurry, okay?"

Danny got out of bed, went to the bathroom, and then put on his favorite Spiderman T-shirt and sweatpants.

Michael stuffed a few day's worth of Danny's clothes in his bag, remembered to grab the hundred and twenty-five dollars he had stashed under his bed and the Visa card his dad finally added his name to in case of emergencies. He then put

Danny's jacket on him and led him down the hallway towards the living room, but stopped before the bend.

The police officers were talking quietly, and he heard their conversation. "We should have just grabbed them." The male cop said.

The woman scoffed, "You don't think their kicking and screaming will attract attention? This way's better. The kid can't know a thing yet. We cut the line before he was told anything."

"Let's just get him to Herrington and we can be done with this."

Michael froze. Herrington? He squeezed his eyes shut, Dobber's voice echoing in his head. Don't trust anyone.

He made a decision he hoped he wouldn't regret. "Be right there," Michael called out. "Just getting some things for Danny."

He grabbed his brother's hand and quickly moved to his parent's bedroom. They had a patio off one wall of their room, which led to the backyard. Michael opened it quietly and led Danny past the pool, the covered fifteen foot motor boat hitched to the jeep and out to the storage shed at the far end of the property.

"Where are Mommy and Daddy?" Danny signed, yawning.

The lie came surprisingly easily. "They had to go away for a while, but they'll be back soon. We need to go somewhere for a little bit."

But where? Suddenly he remembered his old Scout Master, Mr. Mark Jacobs. Michael had been a Boy Scout for years until the age of fourteen and had always liked the guy, trusted him. He would at least know what to do.

As he opened the shed door, Michael smelled his dad's aftershave and a lump formed in his throat. He choked it back and turned to his father's motorcycle stored in the corner. Michael removed the tarp, which covered the bike and picked up two helmets hanging on the rack against the wall.

Danny pulled on his sleeve, his eyes wide. "We're taking Daddy's motorcycle?"

Michael nodded. "Daddy said it was okay." He adjusted the helmet straps to fit Danny's head. After securing the backpack in the travel rack, he hoisted Danny onto the back of the motorcycle.

"Now hold on tight," he signed. Picking up the keys from the cabinet next to him made him pause. Another image of his dad filled his mind, and it was all he could do not to sob. He tried to stop picturing his father teaching him how to drive the bike, against his mother's protests he was too young. It was true, but Gary Anderson always liked to live by his own rules and if he wanted to teach his son something, he did it.

Shaking his head to clear the image, he pushed the motorcycle out of the shed, glancing repeatedly at the house to make sure they weren't seen, and walked it quickly down the dirt road, which ran behind the house. It was an old logging road from the 1850s and luckily for him it was hardly used anymore. The road ran for a half a mile through the woods and then onto the main highway.

The going was slow because the road was muddy and filled with rocks and fallen tree branches. Michael had to stop twice to move some of the larger branches out of the way so he could push the motorcycle through. He finally reached the road, his muscles aching from the effort. When he felt the blacktop under his feet, he got on the bike and started it. Within seconds they were cruising down Route 202 towards Mr. Jacob's house.

He felt better with the cold wind whipping against his face and Danny's little hands gripping his waist. There was something comforting about that. He wanted to tell Danny not to worry, that he would keep him safe, but there was no way to do it at the moment. He felt stupid running from the cops, and he didn't understand anything Dobber had been talking about.

As they passed through town, they stopped at a light. Michael heard a heated conversation coming from the passengers in the car next to him.

"Hey, it's coming on. Be quiet!" someone yelled.

Michael leaned in as the driver turned up the volume on the radio. A news announcer was speaking. "According to the FBI, Hi-Core Industries, the company where kidnapped victims Maddy and Gary Anderson work may be owned by Samuel Herrington or one of his affiliates. The company is vehemently denying any association. There's talk the Anderson's research project, while valid, may be a front and their true agenda is for Herrington himself."

"I told you!" the driver said. "The parents were really doing experiments on their own kid the whole time. Can you believe that?"

A female passenger in the backseat piped up. "Besides being a biophysicist, Herrington's a bioethicist as well. You know, those people all about life and death? He's the one who bought all of the Nazi's doctor's experiment notes, which went on auction last year. Those experiments from The Holocaust where they brought people as close to death as possible and then would bring them back to life? To see if they really could see the afterlife."

"I bet he's doing the same experiments in some secret laboratory now and the parents are using the kid," another woman said.

Michael couldn't remain silent. He turned, leaning towards the car. "Why would you think the Anderson's are working for Herrington?"

The driver glanced at him, his eyebrows raised. "What, you're surprised? The guy has his hands supposedly in nearly every government around the globe. Don't think for a moment he's not involved with us somehow or that he didn't buy out those scientists to work with him behind the scenes. Dirty little spies. Herrington's probably paying them millions."

The light changed green and the car sped forward. Michael sat at the light for a few seconds, frustrated, until someone beeped. He kicked the bike into gear and within minutes came upon Mr. Jacob's house.

He parked the motorcycle, grabbed his knapsack and his brother, and was about to ring the doorbell when Jacobs yanked it open. He glanced around them, his eyes wild and literally grabbed Michael and Danny and pulled them inside.

He slammed shut the door behind him. "Don't say a word," he whispered. He pulled the boys through the ranch house towards the family room in the back, shutting the shades, which looked out to the backyard. Only then did he take a breath, moving them to the table.

"I was hoping you'd come to me."

Michael stared at him, wide-eyed and stunned. "Mr. Jacobs, what's going on?"

Jacobs shook his head, his cell phone ringing. He picked it up, talking and staring at Danny the entire time. Danny had moved over to peer at the saltwater tank set up in the corner of the room.

He nodded. "Yes, they're here. No, no one seemed to have followed them. I know, get here soon."

He clicked it shut. "We need to talk. I have to get you up to speed, and I have to get you up to speed now."

"You know what's happening to us? You know what's happened to my parents?"

Jacobs nodded. "I know everything. Everything about you, your brother, your parents. Even what they were really working on."

Michael's eyes widened. "People are saying my parents work for Herrington. Is that true?" His stomach roiled when Jacobs nodded.

"To an extent." He stared at Michael. "How much do you know?"

"Know?"

"Yeah, know. About your brother. Do you know about the birds? About your parent's research?"

Michael felt like he had left the planet for a few years and come back to people thinking they knew more things about his own brother and family than he did. "I don't know what you're talking about. This has nothing to do with my brother or birds. My parents were just kidnapped by a bunch of crazy terrorists and Dobber, a guy from their lab, called to tell me these same people are after my brother and that the police who came to get us weren't real. I mean, I fled my house with a bunch of cops sitting in my living room. I'm going to get into so much trouble."

Jacobs shook his head, exhaling. "It was a good thing you left. They weren't real policemen." He got up and opened a drawer in a cabinet, taking out a file. "The people who took your parents are after Danny. I've got men coming right now to take you to safety."

Michael was incredulous. "Why would anyone be after a six-year-old deaf kid? And why would they kidnap my parents?" Nothing made sense. "And how do you even know what I'm talking about?" He bordered on panic suddenly.

Jacobs put a reassuring hand on his arm. "Michael, I'm not just your scout leader. I actually work for the FBI and had been assigned to watch out for you and Danny. There are things going on you just don't understand. Things your brother knows."

Michael backed up, scared. He stared at Danny who had moved from the fish tank to a birdcage where a small parakeet chirped. He smiled at it and put his fingers through the bars to play with its feet. The bird twittered and shuffled around happily.

Jacobs opened the file. "What your parents are involved in is complicated. They don't just work at Hi-Core Industries. There are a lot of other things they've dipped their hands into."

"Are they spies or something? That's not true, is it?"

Jacobs nodded, and Michael felt he had been sucker punched. "They are." He waved the file. "Here's the background on your folks, a public file, and I'll just read you the salient facts as quickly as I can. As you know, you have a practically non-existent extended family on each side. Your parents grew up brilliant, graduated at the top of their classes. Both of them went to Columbia and then on to Yale for Graduate school concentrating on pharmacology, biophysics, and chemistry, but after that there is nothing in this file for five years. They vanished off the face of the earth. That's what the news is reporting. People don't just vanish for five years and come back with an excessive amount of cash on them. They must have gotten it from someplace."

"What, they think they were doing something illegal?" Michael asked. They had always been such an open, honest family. There was no way his parents would do something like that.

"Come on, Michael, that's exactly what people are going to think, especially with the connection to Herrington in everyone's mind. They left for five years and when they returned, these seemingly poor scientists with no family or means set up a top-notch research laboratory, including a pharmacology department, moving you to Rockland in a five bedroom house with a pool. Lexus and BMWs in the driveway." Jacobs stared at him. "You were born while they were away you know, but when you moved back, did you ever think where all this newfound money came from? You know scientists don't make that kind of cash regularly."

Michael stood up defensively. "Listen, I don't know what you're implying. You're acting like my parents were drug runners or something. They're not and, no, I never thought about the money. It's not like we're uber-rich. And we moved from a place in Florida to here. People move all the time."

Jacobs stared at him with such pity he was taken aback. "You just think you were living in Florida. Palm trees show up in lots of places." He shook his head. "They should have trusted in you. I told them keeping you in the dark all this time was a bad idea. Dammit!" He slammed his fist on the table and the bird jumped. Danny turned to him, his brow furrowed.

"Look, Herrington has been contacted by our government and of course he's denied having any affiliation with the attack at the plaza. He's blaming it on any of the regional terrorist splinter groups, both domestic and international, which are continuously popping up around the globe. But we know the truth. Your parents were working for him. You have to accept that, but there were reasons. With Herrington's side proclivities leaning towards alternate physics, life, and death and your brother having the ability to know what happens to people when they die, well there's no real stretch to figure why he's after Danny now."

Michael stood up his jaw ajar. "Danny knows what happens to you when you die? Are you out of your mind? He's not the kid from the Sixth Sense! He's just a little deaf kid with a crazy interest in birds, Spiderman, and SpongeBob! You're totally off base." This was too much. Michael turned to his brother and took his hand, trying to smile, to make it seem like everything would be okay, but what he really wanted to do was scream at the top of his lungs.

Jacobs softened a little as a phone rang somewhere else in the house. "I'll be right back. Stay here while I take this call, okay?"

Michael nodded, his head spinning. What if his parents were involved in something illegal, like drugs? Where did they get all their money from and what if his little brother really had some special gifts he didn't know about? It wouldn't be the first time he hadn't noticed something which had been staring him in his face. He turned to Jacob's retreating back, deciding for the moment to give him the benefit of the doubt.

When they were finally alone, Michael turned to face Danny so he could sign to him. Trying to have an in-depth conversation with a six-year-old at any time was hard, but to ask him crazy questions about his parents and ridiculous ideas about the afterlife? He didn't expect this to be easy.

"Danny, did Mommy or Daddy ever talk to you about a guy named Samuel Herrington?"

Danny shook his head, but then Michael didn't think Danny would even know the guy if they had spoken about it.

He had to try a different tack and then remembered the one strange thing he'd heard his mother say before she left last night. The birds in the back of the house. "Danny, I know you like those birds by the house, but I need to know more about them."

Danny looked up worriedly, his eyes filling with tears. "Am I in trouble?"

Michael immediately shook his head. The last thing he wanted to do was scare the kid even more. He needed him calm. "I just need to know about the birds. Are they friendly?"

Danny smiled, more relaxed. "Most of them are," he signed, bouncing up and down on the couch. "Lots of them like SpongeBob, too."

He felt like an idiot having this conversation. Geez, the kid was only six. All six-year-olds liked SpongeBob. "So, they like SpongeBob? Do they watch TV with you?"

"You're silly." Danny giggled. "They don't watch TV anymore. Not after they had to leave their families."

That remark made Michael pause. "What do you mean? Why'd they have to leave their families?"

"Well, they couldn't stay the way they were." Bored with the conversation, Danny jumped up and started exploring the room as Michael sat back on the couch and thought.

He stamped his foot on the ground, getting his brother's attention. "So, you're really just pretending the birds are like people and like SpongeBob and you can play with them, right? That's all it is, a pretend game?"

Danny shook his head. "I'm not pretending. They are people. Mommy and Daddy showed me how to talk to them before they fly away."

"But how can they be people?" Michael asked.

Danny shrugged his shoulders. "Because they just are. They get sick or hurt when they're people and then they turn into birds. That's when I get to talk to them."

Chills ran down his spine when he realized what his brother was actually saying. It was like a horror movie and either his kid brother had a sick sense of humor he didn't know about or someone was feeding him a load of bull. "Danny, you're saying the birds were once living people, just like you or me, before they were birds?"

Danny nodded his head. "And they're my friends until they fly away into the sky." He looked up at the ceiling.

Was this what people thought? What Herrington thought? That his brother could talk to dead people? He started signing again. "Danny, Mommy and Daddy actually told you that you could talk to dead people? And they told you dead people turn into birds? Danny, listen to me. It's not true. People don't turn into birds when they die."

Danny gave him a sly look. "Mommy told me not to tell you because you wouldn't believe us."

Michael tried to swallow this and had a hard time. So many secrets being kept from him. Mr. Jacobs was right. People had lied to him.

"Danny, if this is really true, then how did Mommy and Daddy teach you to talk to them?"

"I've been able to talk to the birds since I was a baby," Danny said. "Mommy just showed me how to send them up to the sky and into the light. I'm a big boy now, and I can help them."

Michael suddenly remembered something. "What about the birds in back of the house. Why are they all burned up? Do you know?"

His brother looked troubled. "I told them I couldn't play with them because Mommy wanted me to stay inside. The birds wouldn't listen and kept flying into the window to try to find me. I told Mommy what was happening and that they were getting hurt, but she kept playing with the machine. She said I had to get stronger to help them. She said the birds were confused and were trying to get to the light through me, but couldn't understand why they couldn't get there. I tried to tell Mommy to stop, that she was making it too strong for them, but she couldn't see me. She kept looking into the machine. It wasn't my fault." Suddenly, his little hands fluttered, and he broke into a sob.

"It's okay, Danny, it's okay," he soothed, patting him on the head. "Hey, no more questions for now, all right?"

Danny nodded and wiped his eyes.

Michael ruffled his hair. "Why don't you go play with that bird again. You guys seem to get along. I'm going to go ask Mr. Jacobs a question."

Michael turned to leave the room, but the sound of gunshots rang out and he flung himself onto Danny, forcing both of them to the floor.

Chapter Four

Samuel Herrington sat stiffly on the sumptuous leather chair, his bejeweled fingers tented, staring through the massive plate glass windows of his corner office and seeing nothing. The rage blinded him to everything, clouding his vision, making him shake. It was so consuming, it was all he could do not to throw something through those windows.

He quieted his mind, letting it wander back to the woman laying on her deathbed in the room down the hall. Attended by no less than a staff of six nurses who changed shifts every four hours, she had the best of everything, yet she asked for nothing.

The air conditioner hissed, so softly it sounded like a young girl sighing and the man closed his eyes. Anyone else would have been awed at the sheer beauty of the scene outside the windows before him, but to him, it was meaningless. On one side, the blue waters of the Pacific Ocean stretched out for miles in every direction. On the other stretched the village with its white walled houses and red stucco roofs adorned with flowering vines.

He stood up from his granite covered desk, counting the fifteen steps it would take to move through the ornate office, ignoring the sculptures that cost more money than ten lifetime's of his cleaning woman's salary. Down the hall of twenty-five steps, adorned with artwork from master painters, past the guards who strolled continuously throughout the property, there solely to protect him. He moved through two fifteen foot chambers, secretaries and messengers shuttling to and from on various errands, each nodding at him respectfully and hurrying on. He opened the door to the suite, and moved quickly the remaining eighteen feet to the bedroom. The nurse glanced at him, and then scurried out.

Samuel stood over the dying woman lying in the stark hospital bed, the white Egyptian silk sheets nearly the color of her skin. Gone was the decadent king-sized headboard with the gold detailing and thick mattress they both had shared. Monitors hummed and beeped, the breathing machine inhaling and exhaling each breath for her. He traced the woman's fingers with his pointer, her skin so fragile he bruised it with his simple touch. Her hand was black and blue from the IV line. Slowly he pulled his hand away and moved to her face.

Her eyes were half open in a drug-induced stupor, yellowed from her poisoned liver seeping its disease into her being. Her scalp showed through her sparse hair, now just wisps of blonde. More strands lay on her pillow. He remembered once when her hair was so thick he couldn't run his fingers through it.

He squinted his eyes and the rage started to build again. He had money. He had power. He had means, yet he had no way to save this woman. At least not on this earth. But maybe he could save her soul.

He turned and fled back to his office, forgetting to count, and picked up the phone, dialing the all too familiar number. He waited mere seconds, then spoke, his voice hard. "Don't make me ask again. Find me the boy, now."

He hung up the phone and stared at the window again, this time glancing to the island off shore where soon his men were bringing the couple. The couple he had nurtured in his beliefs, set up with everything they ever wanted, allowed to have the best of everything as long as they followed his agenda. But they had lied to him.

His rage clouded his vision as he remembered the call.

"Samuel, the Anderson's have been keeping secrets from you. They discovered what happens to you when you die. Their boy knows. It all has to do with the birds that encircle their house. We've got hundreds of photographs proving the connection. They've deceived you."

"Get them here now," he demanded. "And get the kids. Bring them all here."

No one lied to Samuel Herrington.

No one who lived, that was.

Chapter Five

Jacobs flew into the room, his eyes wild. "Come with me." He opened the back door as another round of gunshots riddled the front door.

"What's happening?" Michael yelled, standing and pulling Danny to his feet. The home security alarm went off, squealing shrilly. Danny stared at Michael, frightened, clutching Mr. Teddy tightly in his arms.

"We're being attacked," Jacobs said. "Whoever took your parents knows you're here and they're coming after your brother. Damn tracking device. I didn't know where it was or I would have taken it out myself. Come on. Let's go." He corralled them into the backyard towards the garage. A jeep with tinted windows stood in the driveway. "Get in," Jacobs said, opening the door to the car. He felt inside his pockets. "Damn. I forgot my keys. Get inside and stay down on the floor until I get back. Do you understand? Don't move."

Michael nodded, his body shaking so hard he nearly bit his tongue.

Jacobs turned, now with a gun in his hands and ran back to the house. Michael pushed Danny into the back seat floor well and covered him with his own body.

"What's happening?" Danny asked.

Michael had never seen his brother so terrified. Thank God Danny couldn't hear the gunshots. He knew it was no time to lie to him. It was too important he understand the danger they were in. He signed quickly. "Danny, someone is mad at Mom and Dad and now they're trying to find us. They're in Mr. Jacob's house right now, and we need to hide from them until they leave. Don't worry, we'll be safe here." He leaned over and locked the car doors as he heard another volley of gunshots erupt from the house and covered his brother with his body.

There was a loud commotion and the sound of angry voices.

"Where the hell did they go?" a man yelled.

A woman replied. "I'm sure they're nearby. Michael's jacket is still in the house."

The voices came closer, and the woman chastised the man, "Jacobs probably got them away right before we came in. What were you thinking, shooting him?"

The voices halted in front of the car. "I was just doing my job. You want to be the one to tell Herrington they got away again? We should have grabbed them in the house rather than sitting in their living room passively with the kid making us look like idiots. Now we'll have to wait until we pick up the signal again. This is wasting time."

It was the cops from his house. Dobber was right. They were fakes. He heard the woman try the locks on the car and then saw her lean in, trying to see past the tinted windows.

Danny, please don't move, Michael prayed silently, when suddenly Michael heard a bird screeching and the woman screamed. "Get it away from me."

"Carol, will you move and let me shoot the damned bird already?"

"Garrett, you know who this is?" Carol spoke up. "This is probably Jacobs. You know, the guy you offed a few minutes ago thinking you were just doing your job? It's why I told you not to kill anyone in any way connected to the kid. You were just supposed to scare them into giving them to us."

Michael heard him pause and then a gunshot made him jump. He stiffened when he heard Danny utter a muffled cry.

The woman spoke. "Good, at least he can't help them now. Do me a favor and listen to me, you got that? Don't make me tell Herrington how many times you screwed up. You follow the plan as it's been laid out, you hear me? Now, let's get out of here before all of Jacobs' friends show up. The kids probably went back down Route 202 towards town, and we can intercept them there. Keep everyone tuned in to their radios and have them contact us as soon as they hear anything. They can't go far in this town anymore without someone noticing them. We'll just wait until the locals find them and follow their trail, or wait until we pick up the signal again." There was a pause as a sound of an engine rumbled in the driveway. "Ah, good, they're here."

Car doors slammed and the car revved and retreated down the graveled driveway. Michael refused to move until he heard nothing but silence. Only then did he crane his neck and peep out the car window, watching the back of an unmarked brown sedan fade from view. He heard sirens in the distance. Michael turned and uncovered Danny. His brother had tears streaming down his face.

"They shot your scout master, didn't they?" Danny signed.

Michael had no idea how Danny could know this. "Yeah, they killed him," he signed, devastated his brother had to hear it.

Danny shook his head. "No, he's not dead yet. We have to hurry. I have to help him before he really dies."

Confused, Michael opened the door and they both climbed out. Danny solemnly walked over to where a plump pigeon was lying on the ground, drawing its last breath. Blood slowly trickled from its beak. Danny bent down to it.

Michael was about to stop him, but instead watched dumbstruck as his brother gently picked up the bird. As he held it, Michael could swear he saw a thin sliver of light spring up from Danny's hand and surround the bird. It lasted for only an instant, but he was certain it had been there. He would have bet his three Derek Jeter rookie cards on it.

He inched over to Danny, who mumbled to the critically injured animal, and watched as the pigeon took its final breath and died in his hands.

"He's okay," Danny signed. He walked over and laid the bird in the tall grass by the edge of the road. "I saved him."

Did he just see what he thought he saw? "What did you just do?"

"I just sent Mr. Jacobs away like Mommy showed me," he said. "He tried to help us, but those bad men shot him and almost killed him. I had to send him away to the light before he died."

It was like trying to take a final exam in advanced calculus when he had never even learned addition. Michael couldn't understand anything. He had to learn the truth. "Danny, Mr. Jacobs died in his house. I heard the bad people say they shot him."

Danny shook his head. "No, you don't understand. He really almost died when the bad men shot him when he was a bird. I had to send him away before that happened. Otherwise, he never would've found his way home. Not for a long, long time."

I'm losing it, Michael thought. Suddenly, he was aware of sirens coming closer. A helicopter sounded in the distance. For a second he hesitated, wondering if they should stay, if these were the people Jacobs had told him were coming for him. But then he remembered the fear in Dobber's voice, telling him to flee, to trust no one.

"Danny, we have to go now," he said. "I hear people." He grabbed his backpack and his brother's hand and raced into the woods behind Mr. Jacob's house. "We're going to have to stay out of sight for awhile until I think of what to do next, okay?"

Danny nodded.

What had Mom and Dad done to him? This little kid who was petrified of spiders, sleeping in the dark, and anything with scaly green skin, seemed to have no problem picking up a dying bird covered in blood. He was shocked his parents had apparently conducted some experiments on Danny, not to mention that little bomb of information about his parents working for Samuel Herrington. Thoughts of bio-agents, espionage, and his parents being tortured rattled through his brain and he tried to push them aside. They were too horrible to contemplate.

He and Danny walked for miles, stopping every once in a while to allow Danny to rest. Michael couldn't stop looking behind him, terrified they were being followed. He thought he heard dogs barking once or twice and wondered if a canine unit was after them. That spurred him on.

He remembered there was a small motel located near the highway. It had a seedy reputation, but he figured it would be safe enough for them to hole up in, until he worked out what his next move should be. The motel was right where he thought it would be, about five hundred yards ahead.

A tinny bell clanged as they entered the cramped front office, which reeked of sweat and tobacco. Michael told Danny to stand behind him and keep his head down while he paid cash for the room for one night. He shouldn't have worried about them being recognized from the news because the guy at the desk hardly even glanced up from his racing forms. He took Michael's money and handed him the keys to Room 19.

"The room is at the end of the walkway, second floor, make a left," he said, coughing. A chewed up, smelly cigar dangled from his lips.

"Thanks," Michael mumbled. He grabbed the keys, ushered Danny upstairs, and into the room.

Danny scrunched up his nose. "Is this where we're going to stay?"

"No, Birdman, we'll be here just for a little while." He grimaced. The place was a dump. Michael tore his gaze away from the stains on the bedspread, trying not to imagine what they really were. He moved throughout the room, taking in the scratches on the furniture and the pile of dead cockroaches lying in the corner.

The bathroom was no better, and the lingering scent of urine reminded him of the boy's bathroom at his school at the end of the day. At least there the janitor sprayed an orange smelling disinfectant each night, so it was reasonably clean the next day. Michael didn't think this bathroom had seen or felt the touch of a sponge or soap in quite a while.

The only saving grace in the room was a twenty-two inch color flat-screen in the corner. He saw the wires protruding from its back and was pleasantly surprised to see they had cable. At least he could keep Danny occupied until he could figure out what to do.

His stomach growled. "Hey, you hungry?" He realized they hadn't eaten since the night before.

Danny nodded enthusiastically.

"Okay, I'm going to run down the hall to the vending machines. You and Mr. Teddy stay here and I'll be right back. Here, you can watch TV." Michael turned it on. Jimmy Neutron was just starting. Great timing. He locked Danny in and ran down the walkway.

Within minutes he had Danny were engrossed in a great episode where, once again, Jimmy was saving the world from chaos, and Michael had time to finally catch his breath. He split between the two of them whatever he could find, a package of Twinkies, Oreo cookies, a bag of potato chips, and a grape soda.

Michael glanced at his brother guiltily. So much for being responsible. "Danny, don't tell Mommy I fed you this, okay? She'll kill me."

Danny giggled around a mouthful of chocolate cookie.

After the show was over, Michael saw Danny was getting tired, so he lay with him on the bed. He tried to rest, but he couldn't. He kept thinking about the machine Danny had mentioned back at Mr. Jacobs' house.

Just thinking about Jacobs made a lump form in his throat. The man had died for him and Danny. Never in a million years would Michael think he would be one of those people folks read about in the paper. Parents kidnapped, involved in illegal activity. People after him. People giving their lives for him. It was so hard to fathom.

He tried to remember seeing any unfamiliar machines or equipment at his house, but he couldn't recall any. He felt left out and alone as he lay there. What else had his parents not let him in on? What other secrets would he uncover before his parents were found? Even with all the unanswered questions running through his head, his body finally gave in and he drifted off to an exhausted sleep.

Day 2 Tuesday, 6:30 p.m.

Michael awoke abruptly to the phone ringing. Disoriented after a mid-day nap, he stared at it stupidly for two more rings before he picked up the receiver. "Hello?" His mouth felt like he had cotton stuffed in it.

"Michael, it's Dobber. Turn on the television." He recognized Dobber's voice immediately.

Michael came fully awake. His gaze flew around the room. "Dobber, how did you find us here?"

"Don't worry about that," he said. "It isn't me you should be worrying about. I've had a lock on your brother ever since he was a baby. Now turn on ABC."

Michael quickly moved to the television and turned it on. Another day of chaos had ripped through the world. He watched an aerial broadcast of a terrible fire engulfing a home. Police cars were everywhere and firefighters battled a terrific blaze going on at an adjacent house, where the fire had spread.

"Do you see now why you had to leave the house?" Dobber said. "Why those people who came for you weren't to be trusted?"

Realization and horror dawned on him when he recognized what he was looking at. "Oh, my, God. That's my house. What happened?"

Dobber's voice was tight with anger. "They blew it up."

Michael flinched as the shed in the backyard burst into flames.

"My guess is your parents aren't cooperating so their captors are making a point. If you have nowhere to go, they figure it'll be easier for them to pick you up."

Michael pulled his eyes away from the screen. "How do you know all this? Aren't you just a guy who works with my parents at Hi-Core? How are you finding us?" Michael glanced around the room, patted his body, thinking maybe there was a camera or tracer attached to him someplace.

Dobber took a deep breath. "Michael, it's true, I work at the lab with your parents, but we're more than just casual acquaintances. I've been friends with your parents since college, and the three of us ended up working at the same company when we graduated. When Herrington came to us and made us an offer, it was one none of us could refuse. The money alone was enough to give anyone pause, but the ability to have our own labs and do our own research? It's a scientist's dream." He paused, and Michael's worst fears were confirmed. His skin crawled, and he couldn't find his voice.

Dobber continued. "A year before Danny was born we realized the money Herrington was giving us to help him wasn't worth the jeopardy we were putting our country in. You were already ten years old and your parents were so afraid for you. When you have children, your priorities change. Your parents were my best friends, so the three of us defected, so to speak."

"So, my parents are spies."

Dobber responded quickly. "Were spies, Michael, but not anymore. They made a conscious decision to break with the organization. Right before Danny was born your mother and father stopped sending their research results or any other secret information to Herrington's people. In fact, they sent faulty documentation. They were terrified what they discovered would end up in his hands. Deception was the only way."

"So, Herrington really is a bad guy?" Michael asked.

"As bad as it gets," Dobber said. "The man has his hands in the back pockets of many countries, and stays there by threatening to poison their water supply or make their entire population sterile with any one of his number of bio-chemical agents in his arsenal. Herrington wanted your parents to inform him of any new discoveries or antidotes the United States was working on, but even more important than that was their experiments on the afterlife. Ever since Herrington was a young man, he was always pre-occupied with death. But now the ante is upped. His wife is dying, and he knows your parents have been working over the past few years on side experiments about death and the afterlife.

"And then your brother was born and your parents realized he already had the very gift they were seeking. The experiment wasn't in any lab, but in your brother, so they felt there was no other choice and began using their discoveries and techniques on Danny. It was the only way they could be sure their theories were correct and keep the information out of Herrington's hands, who would exploit it for his own selfish purposes."

Michael was trying to wrap his head around everything he was hearing. Experiments on his brother, his parents aligned with the biggest bad guy in the world. "But what happened? Why were they kidnapped?"

Dobber raised his voice and Michael could picture him, his round face red in the cheeks. "Everything went wrong. Even with the fail safes and protocols we put in place, Herrington's people found out somehow."

"What did my parents do to my brother?" Michael whispered, afraid to know. "Did they make him deaf?"

Dobber's reply was hesitant, tense. "That was an accident. When your mother was pregnant with him, she was in the midst of a research project using ultraviolet rays as an alternative light therapy method. The machine she was working on malfunctioned, sending an intense amount of ultraviolet activity throughout the room. She collapsed, and it took your father and me nearly three hours to get her out of there because she had locked the door from the inside."

A memory flickered. "So, that's what happened when I was eleven."

"You know about it?" Dobber asked, surprise registering in his tone.

"Yeah, some of it. I remember my mother was home for weeks. They said she'd fallen and hit her head," Michael said. "So, how'd they figure out the connection between Danny and the birds?"

"Whenever your mother brought him to the lab while she worked on the ultraviolet experiments, he'd react very strangely, making nonsense sounds to the air and smiling out the window. We finally started noticing the birds and the correlation. Your parents didn't really do anything to him he couldn't do himself. They just heightened his awareness. It wasn't until he was old enough to communicate that your parents discovered the true meaning of his abilities."

Michael glanced at his brother, sleeping innocently in the king-sized bed. He seemed so small. "What about this light everyone keeps talking about?"

"Okay," Dobber said. "I'm going to try to explain this in the least scientific way possible. Just try to keep an open mind. When your parents were hired by Herrington, it wasn't to just work on a cure for Alzheimer's disease or Parkinson's disease. They were sent with two agendas. The first was to send Herrington information on what the Americans were working on, what new antidotes they were discovering, things of a bio-chemical nature. The real job, though, was to find out what happens to people when they die. Everyone talks about seeing a bright light. Your parents' job was to find the true meaning of the light, and they were to go to any ends to explore all the techniques and experiments that were available and to report any findings back to Herrington."

Michael was livid. "So, the research on light therapy for seniors was always a lie, right? Everything has been a complete lie, hasn't it?" One moment he was a regular kid, babysitting his brother, and now he was running for his life, the son of traitors who had sold themselves to a maniacal despot who wanted to rule the world and was trying to capture him and Danny. As much as he desperately wanted to find his parents, he was so angry at them. It was as if he were suddenly living with a group of strangers.

Dobber must have sensed Michael's anger. "Michael, you weren't told the truth about your parents because they were trying to protect you. As for their research on light therapy for seniors, it was real and they really were receiving an award at the Plaza for their work. They had to be working on something legitimate all these years so they wouldn't be discovered by agents in the United States and sent to jail. You should be proud of them for that. This award was an incredible accomplishment.

"The problems began last month when Herrington learned your parents actually discovered what the true light was and were withholding it from him. Herrington sent someone to discuss this with them, and of course they denied discovering any true reason for the light, but Herrington didn't believe them." Dobber paused, took another deep breath and continued. "So, Herrington ordered a raid on the lab where we worked, and when it came up empty, they went through your house. The problem was, for a long time Herrington didn't know the research wasn't to be found in any computer banks or files. It was in your brother. Danny is the key, and only Danny can unlock the mysteries of the light.

Herrington's people have been secretly photographing your family, and all of the birds, which have been mysteriously appearing at your home for the past month. It was only a matter of time before he put two and two together, concluding your parents either defected or were being coerced from another source. Either way, he's desperate, so he had to move fast. Time is not something he has. He assumed you both would be at the Plaza with your folks when they were being presented with the award. Otherwise, he would have simply picked you up that night while your parents were away."

Michael could barely speak, but managed a strangled whisper. "What if that's not the answer? What if someone told them what my parents were doing?"

Dobber grunted. "I've racked my brains for hours on end and can't come up with a single person who could do that."

Michael was still suspicious. "So how do you fit into this, Dobber? Why haven't the police or the FBI come after you? They must think you're in on this, too."

"I'm not the one who snitched on your folks," he said vehemently. "I'm in as much danger as they are. Herrington's people did come after me, right after they attacked the Plaza. As soon as I heard about the attack, I took all the loose data, the machine, and the tracking devices straight to a secret lab we never registered with Herrington or under any of our names. It's where I've been hiding. You have to trust me. I'm in just as much danger as you." He paused again. "Listen,

Michael, you need to bring Danny to me. I can keep him safe."

"Really?" Michael asked sarcastically. "No offense, but I don't trust you anymore either, Dobber. You were a spy too. You've been lying to me as much as my folks all these years, so what makes you think I should believe you now?" He paused. "Want me to trust you? Tell me about the tracking device. The one you say you've had on my brother since he was born."

Dobber replied eagerly. "Your parents implanted a small microchip in his inner ear. It is completely harmless, but we can locate him to the tenth of a mile so if he ever got into the wrong hands we could get to him. When I see you, I'll be able to explain everything and I'll take out the microchip so he won't be tracked again. Don't try to do it yourself, it's very dangerous and could cause permanent damage."

Okay, he was finally getting some information. He still didn't trust this guy, but maybe Dobber would tell him some more. "One more thing, you didn't explain about the birds. Danny says they're people. That's not really true, is it?"

Dobber laughed, and he finally sounded a little like the happy-go-lucky guy Michael remembered. "You seem to know a lot for someone who knew almost nothing twenty-four hours ago. Yes, we believe birds are people. Or, actually are people's souls, if you want to be more specific. Over the last few years we learned birds are not really what you and the rest of the world think they are. All birds are simply vessels of the newly deceased. Your parents, with Danny's help, have discovered that when we die in our human bodies, our souls become one with the birds. It is the first step before we are ready to meet the light. The Light of Heaven. In nearly every religion, there is a version of Heaven, a paradise realm, and though people believe in faith in this garden of eternity, the ability to physically understand it is an exceptional gift."

"Wait, you're saying my brother can see Heaven?" he asked.

"I'm saying Danny has exceptional abilities and can see the light," Dobber answered. "He has the power to talk to the souls within the birds and send them on their way to Heaven. The version of Heaven which is the vision of every religion."

"Oh really?" Michael said. "Tell me, Dobber, what did they do before Danny was around? Are you telling me that all the birds in the land were just waiting for my little brother to be born before they could go to Heaven? That's the stupidest thing I ever heard. Why don't you just tell me then that Danny is the new messiah and then maybe you can get all the religious cults to believe you, too."

"No, that's not it, Michael. Not at all. Everything happened as it does now but no one knew. Don't you understand? No one ever even conceived of this type of concept. Think of the possibilities! When we die in our human bodies, we're not really dead. Our souls are just transferred before we finally leave this world and go to Heaven. But, imagine if you knew which people became what birds and you could stop them from finding the light. What power you would have. Anyone who had the power to determine who would and would not go to Heaven would be the most powerful being in the universe. They would be akin to God. That's what Herrington wants. It's not money. It's not fame. It's power. If he could determine whose soul was whose? What person wouldn't do anything to make sure their loved ones moved on? His wife, Marta, is dying, but he's hoping he can keep her soul a bit more, or at the very least, guarantee her soul moves on to the next realm."

Michael still wasn't convinced. "Okay, but just how did my parents make this connection? How did they figure out which birds were which?"

"Listen, we're still working on this project and I can't go into it anymore," Dobber said impatiently. "I need to get to you and your brother. Now, I want you to wait there. I can be in New York by tomorrow morning. Unfortunately, I can't leave yet or I'll arouse suspicion. So, in the meantime, stay in the hotel, close your blinds and I'll get to you by noon, okay? Remember, I have the tracer, but it'll be harder to find you if you're moving around. Will you do this for me? For your brother?"

Did he have much of a choice? Maybe Dobber really was what he said. He'd given Michael more information than anyone so far. "Sure, I can do that, I guess."

He heard Dobber take a relieved breath. "Good, that's very good," he said. "Trust me, Michael, you're doing the right thing. I promise we'll talk more when I see you." He hung up the phone.

Michael turned back to the news. His house had burnt to the ground, and the firefighters were extinguishing the last of the flames. The newscasters showed Danny and Michael's school pictures and asked anyone who had seen them last to please alert the authorities. He could imagine what his friends thought.

"Well, I guess this is my fifteen minutes of fame," Michael thought grimly.

He shut off the TV and turned to his brother, who was stirring.

Michael stretched his legs and moved over to the window, pulling the curtain back. Two sedans were pulling up across the street. One of the doors opened and two policemen jumped out, moving quickly to the front office. Michael immediately recognized the male and female police officers from his house. But how could they possibly have found them? The only person who knew where they were was Dobber.

Realization hit him and he smacked his hand to his forehead. He was such an idiot. Dobber was still working for Herrington and had used the motel phone, or the device in Danny's ear, to track them. Served him right for thinking he could trust someone. Michael flew to the bed, shaking Danny fully awake.

Then he went and glanced back out the window and watched as two more officers got out of the other sedan and started to move briskly towards the front office.

"Michael, what's the matter?" Danny signed, alarmed. "Are the bad men here?"

Michael nodded, his face grim. "Yeah, come on, we have to get out of here." Danny jumped up and Michael grabbed his knapsack, his brother, and slowly opened the door. He peeked over the side rail on the right side and saw the fake cops come out of the front office and start for the stairs, guns drawn. Michael quickly locked the door to delay them and then made a left down a short hallway which ran around to the back of the motel. There was a staircase at the end and they bolted down it, leading them straight into the back parking lot. Behind the lot, about two hundred yards away, was a five store strip mall. Michael heard a commotion behind him, heard the officers pounding on the door. This was followed immediately by a loud gunshot and the sound of the doorjamb ripping apart. Heart pounding, Michael grabbed

Danny's hand, and they made a mad dash across the lot and into the first of the strip stores.

It was a 7-Eleven. The smell of antiseptic cleansers, microwave burritos, and coffee assaulted his senses. A bell announced his entrance and he tried not to flinch. Calming himself down as best he could, he strolled casually to the counter. "Hey, you have a bathroom around here? My brother really has to go."

The teen behind the counter with his red Mohawk and multi-pierced ears yawned and pointed towards the back of the store. "Yeah, dude. Go through there, past the staircase."

"Thanks." Michael took a quick glance back at the motel and saw the cops standing at the bottom of the steps, glancing around. Abruptly, the female officer moved a few feet in their direction and stopped. She bent down and picked up something lying on the ground.

Michael thought he was going to be sick. It was Mr. Teddy.

Herrington's agents immediately started towards the stores at a brisk pace. Without waiting to see anything further Michael grabbed Danny's hand and dragged him to the back rooms, seeing the staircase the attendant had mentioned. He hoped it connected to some of the other stores on the strip or to a back door. Ignoring the bathroom, Michael raced down the steps. Just as he reached the bottom rung, he heard the bell. The agents were in the store.

Michael dashed through a narrow hallway, stacked high with boxes, and came to a metal door. It was locked. He threw his weight against it, but nothing happened.

He froze as he heard Garrett talking to the counter clerk.

"Look at this photo. You see these two kids come in here?"

"No, I didn't see them. Why, what'd they do?"

Michael was shocked. The kid's protecting us!

Garrett apparently wasn't buying his line. "I'm going to let you take another look and ask you again. Have you seen them?"

"I told you I didn't see anyone," the clerk yelled. "You know, this store is taped. You can't threaten me or I'll sue you for police brutality."

A sudden single gunshot blast shook the walls, followed by a deafening silence.

Michael's paralysis broke. Frantically, he searched the room and noticed a rotting piece of wood covering a narrow, dank crawlspace under the stairs. "Danny, come here. The bad men are here." Danny ran over to him, whimpering.

Michael knew Danny hated the dark. Knew he wouldn't be able to see him to sign to him.

"I know this is scary, but please don't be afraid. We have to go in there right now. You have to be brave, Birdman. I promise you, I'll be right behind you." Danny wouldn't move, and Michael had no choice. He picked him up and pushed him through the hole, kicking and screaming.

He heard the agents start down the stairs.

Michael pushed his way into the crawlspace behind his brother and shoved the wood into place.

Danny threw himself onto Michael's back, digging his fingers into his skin. Michael knew he was terrified. He turned him and hugged him and then, in the dark, as he couldn't sign, he put his hand over his mouth and then over Danny's ears. His brother thankfully quieted, but still whimpered softly.

As his eyes adjusted to the darkness he noticed a faint light about fifty feet ahead. The crawlspace was only about four feet high, so taking Danny by the hand, they half-crawled, half-walked through dirt and rotted pieces of wood towards the light.

Halfway to the light source he abruptly stopped, holding Danny in place and covering his mouth with his hands again. He turned around and saw the filtering light from the storage room, but froze when one of the police officers removed the wood covering the crawl space. He was never so happy in his life to be sitting in almost total darkness.

"Do you think they went in here?" someone asked.

"Probably, you idiot. Get me a flashlight," the woman said, peering into the crawlspace. Michael knew she couldn't see them, but it seemed as if she stared right at him. Without waiting for someone to get her a flashlight, Michael pushed Danny quietly along and in a few more seconds they were up against a mesh wire covering which let them out in the back lot of the strip mall. He pushed Danny gently to one side and then using all his strength, Michael kicked in the mesh. It was old and fell off its hinges with two more swift kicks. He dropped Danny through the vent and followed him, just as a flashlight beam glided by them.

They hit the pavement, and Michael grabbed Danny and ran to the far side of the strip mall and across the street into the woods.

"Where are we going?" Danny signed, crying. He was covered in dust.

Michael sighed, wiping a small spot of blood off of his arm where he had cut it coming out of the crawlspace. He turned and brushed the dust out of Danny's hair. "I don't know, yet. We're just going to have to keep moving."

Michael pulled Danny along through several miles in the backwoods of their hometown, all the while staring back, expecting to see the police officers running through the woods after them. Danny complained about all the walking, dragging his feet and Michael had to push him forward, making empty promises of rewards he would get for listening. Promises he was sure he wasn't going to be able to keep. Finally, he recognized where they were and moved them along a path, which led to a local horse farm. It was the

McKenna property and Michael had a great working knowledge of the place, having dated Becky McKenna his entire sophomore and junior year in high school, right up until her dad had accepted a corporate job in Raleigh a few months before. As far as he knew, the farm still hadn't been sold, so it was empty. Score one for him and the bad economy.

The McKenna's had raised thoroughbreds and as they passed by the deserted stables, towards the farmhouse, he was struck again by its size. It reminded him of the great Victorian houses from the literature books he'd read in English class. He remembered Becky teaching him about the trick lock to the basement door at the back of the house, the one that used to be used by servants in the old days. You just had to jiggle the knob at the same time you put pressure on the lower panel and the door would pop open. On quite a few occasions he had used this technique to sneak in to see Becky while her parents thought she was doing her homework.

The basement was finished and the blue carpet was as thick as he remembered, though the moldy smell which pervaded the house was something Mrs. McKenna would never have allowed. He saw the source of the smell on the wall next to him. Brown water stains streaked down the white walls and the carpet below them was discolored and warped from water damage.

"Let's go upstairs." He brought Danny up to the first floor and checked the thermostat. He was pleasantly surprised the electricity hadn't been turned off and, though he had no intention of turning on the lights and calling attention to them, he certainly had no problem turning the heat on. April nights were still cold in Rockland.

They moved to the second floor and into the master bathroom. Michael signed to Danny. "Come over here, Birdman. I need to look in your ears." He risked turning on the bathroom light so he could see.

Danny flopped in front of him, exhausted. His eyes were half closed.

Michael first checked in his left ear and didn't see anything. He wasn't quite sure he even knew what he was searching for. Still, if Dobber was telling the truth, then there had to be some sort of tracking device on him or how else could they have been located two different times already? But then, why would Dobber have told him the truth in the first place if he were one of Herrington's agents?

For lack of any other ideas, Michael ran his fingers through Danny's hair, made him open his mouth, checked his teeth and then tried the other ear. He pulled the lobe out a bit so he could look into the canal, and then he saw what he was searching for. Just inside the canal was a small metal microchip, the size of a Tic-Tac, but much flatter.

Dobber had been telling the truth. Why?

Michael turned back to his brother. "Danny, I don't want you to be worried, but you have something in your ear."

Danny yawned. "You mean my robot parts?"

He was surprised. "You know what's in your ear?"

Danny nodded. "Mommy says I'm like a superhero and it makes me strong. She takes it out and fixes it sometimes. I'm just like Spiderman." He pointed to his idol on his shirt.

So many secrets. His own mother had a tracking device on him. Just how dangerous did everyone think his brother was? He cocked his head and started signing again. "Danny, how does Mommy take it out? Does it hurt when she does it?" He remembered Dobber talking about permanent damage if he tried to remove it, but didn't believe him.

Danny scrunched up his face. "It hurts a little but Mommy pulls it out with a metal thing. She says I'm a really brave boy."

"Yeah, you are a brave kid." If his mother could take it out, then he could do it, too. There was no way he was going to allow Dobber or his people to find his brother again if he could help it. Michael pulled a Swiss army knife out of a side pocket of his knapsack. It was one of the master knives with everything from forks and spoons to a fishing hook and of course, tweezers.

Michael took out the tweezers and tilted his brother's head towards the light. "Bet you didn't expect us to get away, did you, Dobber?" Michael whispered, concentrating on directing the tweezers into Danny's ear without hurting him. He felt like he was playing the kid's game Operation.

The microchip was within the tweezers' grasp, and he pulled on it gently. He could see just one hair-thin suture connecting the chip to Danny's ear canal. What he needed was a minute pair of scissors, but since he didn't have one, and was scared to use one of the knives, he decided to just pull it out. He took a deep breath and yanked on it. The suture snapped easily, and Danny cried out.

"Did I hurt you?" Michael asked, grimacing.

Danny made a face and held his hand to his ear. "Mommy does it a lot better."

"I'm sorry." Michael checked his ear again and saw that the small tear was already clotting. He then examined the microchip in the tweezers with disgust before placing it on the floor. He moved Danny out of the way and then stamped on it with his shoe. When it didn't shatter, he grabbed a piece of tile that was loose on the wall and smashed it onto the chip. It broke into five neat pieces and Michael struck them repeatedly until they were completely crushed. Afterwards, he dumped all the pieces into the toilet and flushed them away, only then breathing a sigh of relief.

"We're going to be okay for the moment, Danny."

Danny was frowning at him, his arms crossed across his chest.

"What?" Michael asked.

"Why did you smash up my superhero parts?"

Michael stifled a grin. "Mom would want me to do that. They weren't working anymore. As soon as we find her we'll get you new parts. I promise."

In one of the bedrooms there was an old couch the McKenna's had abandoned. Michael lay down on it and let Danny crawl into his arms. After a minute, Danny looked up sadly and signed, "Did the bad men take Mr. Teddy?"

He sighed. "Yeah, they did. We dropped him back at the hotel. I'm really sorry, Danny."

Instead of crying, Danny gave Michael a brave smile. "It's okay. I'm a big boy. Mr. Teddy was for babies." He lay back on Michael's chest. "And anyway, at least Mr. Teddy still has his robot parts."

Michael smiled. A real one for the first time in days. Two tracking devices and both gone. Now no one should be able to locate them and they were truly on their own.

Michael patted Danny's back until he fell asleep, not having any idea what the morning would bring.

Chapter Six

The lab was a marvel in design. Crisp white walls and floors, white tables jam-packed with such a wide array of scientific equipment it would put an entire university's facilities to shame. At least fifty technicians were working painstakingly, peering over beakers, Bunsen burners, measuring, calibrating. It was cold in this room, the experiments going on needed to be kept at near freezing levels so the chemicals didn't combust.

Herrington held a pipette and squeezed the contents from a beaker into a test tube, giving instructions to a group of scientists in orange bio-hazard uniforms. Nodding, they gently took the test tube and left the room, moving through to the quarantine area. The hiss of the doors as they traversed from one room to the other was background noise to an opera by Wagner which wafted softly through the wall speakers.

"Mr. Herrington, you have a call." A masked and gowned aide appeared at his side, holding a cellphone.

Herrington removed his face mask and gloves and stared at the man. The aide didn't look him in the eye and with good reason. If Herrington was in a specific mood and he thought you were staring at him the wrong way, you might end up puking your guts up for days thinking your tuna sandwich had gone bad, but never really knowing the truth.

Herrington took the phone. "Yes? You have them yet?" When he didn't hear what he wished, he stormed the fifty-five feet out of the lab, down a long hallway of sixty-three feet, through a set of French doors and onto the patio where he collapsed into a plush lawn chair. Within seconds he was handed a glass of ice tea, fresh with five pieces of crushed mint and fifteen ice cubes in the shape of perfect marble sized orbs.

Herrington's voice was livid. "What do you mean they got away? They're children! A naive seventeen-year-old kid and his six-year-old deaf brother. How many times has this been, Carol? I put you on this mission for a reason! Are you telling me you and your men can't keep two little boys in your midst? Don't call me again until you have something to report, you hear me? If not I'll take all of you off the case immediately and find someone who can get the job done right."

He called to his aide. "Go to the news and put out an APB on these kids. Weave the story they killed Jacobs and the 7-Eleven clerk. That they're armed and dangerous. Put a bounty on their heads of five million dollars and say it's coming from Hi-Core Industries—that they're devastated about the traitors in their midst and will do anything to bring about justice. Trust me, the kids won't be missing for long."

The aide nodded and scurried away to make his calls. Herrington took a sip of the iced tea. It had melted in the time it took him to speak to Carol and his rage was starting to mount again. He closed his eyes and breathed deeply as his assistant anticipated this, handing him another fresh tea. He took it and drank deeply.

Things were going according to plan as long as they got the kids. The parents were in his custody and nearly at the facility. He smiled as he remembered telling his men to soften them up for him before they got there. Gary Anderson wouldn't be so cocky after they were done. He had never liked the guy.

Chapter Seven

Day 3 Wednesday 9:15 a.m.

Michael and Danny woke to a warm room, the sun streaming through the windows, and the sound of voices coming from downstairs. If there had been eggs frying on the stove and the smell of coffee and bacon in the air, Michael would have sworn he was home.

Instead of his mother's warm voice calling him to breakfast, a nasal, high-pitched soprano reached his ears.

"Oh, you're just going to love this place. It's really a beautiful home, perfect for children. Come, you've just got to see the country kitchen."

The question was, should they remain hidden, or see if these people could help them? The visitors downstairs certainly didn't sound like the people after them, so Michael took a chance. Rubbing his eyes and yawning, he shook Danny gently awake. "Come on, Birdman. We have to go."

He and Danny stumbled their way downstairs.

Just as they reached the bottom steps an older, bleached-blonde woman with too-red lips and a couple in their thirties strolled into the foyer. When Michael saw the couple's wide eyes and dropped jaws, it completely destroyed any hope they wouldn't be recognized.

The older woman, on the other hand, seemed clueless. She perched her hands on her ample hips and frowned. "How did you boys get in here? The front door was locked. Did you break in? You know, I should call the police on you."

Michael put up his hands and tried to sound sincere. "I'm really sorry. We didn't break anything. There's a trick door in the basement. I used to know the people who lived here, and my brother and I needed a safe place to stay."

The husband nudged his wife in the ribs, but spoke to Michael. "You guys are those kids who've been all over the news, aren't you?"

Michael nodded.

The man moved forward and extended his hand. "My name's Rick Somers and this is my wife, Cathy."

Michael grabbed his outstretched hand. "We have been trying to find someone to help us, but every place we go we get attacked. Do you think you could help us get to the FBI or something?"

"Of course, anything we can do to help," Rick said. "Cathy, we should take them to our house until we figure out what to do. Come on, guys, the car's outside." He turned to the broker. "Sorry, Sylvia, we'll have to come back another time. Do us a favor and don't tell anyone they're with us, okay? And don't sell the house to anyone else. We'll take it. It's perfect."

Michael would have laughed at Sylvia's shocked expression, but Rick was already hustling them out of the house and into his car. Rick kept glancing around nervously when they were outside and Michael couldn't blame him for being scared. They were wanted people. Still, things were moving fast and for a second he was unsure if they should go with the Somerses. His paranoia was in full swing and he was questioning everything and everyone, even if it was hope handed to him on a silver platter. He hung back from getting into the car.

Rick glanced over and saw Michael's hesitation. "What's the matter? Is everything okay? You see something?" He tried to peer behind Michael, his hands clenched.

"Everything's just moving so quickly."

Rick grimaced, chagrined and took a deep breath, opening his hands. "I'm sorry, it's like I'm kidnapping you, too, aren't I? It's just Sylvia is having an open house here in less than a half an hour, and I didn't want you guys to be here when a whole throng of people showed up. I'm just being overly cautious and no offense, kid, but I don't want to be the next target your buddies decide to come after if they somehow find out you're with us. I'd feel a lot safer on my home turf." He smiled sheepishly. "Just call me Bond. James Bond."

Michael stared at him for a moment and felt the tension finally leave his body. The guy seemed genuine. He had to stop thinking everyone in the world was out to get them. "I'm sorry. It's just after all we've been through, I'm trying to be careful." He brought Danny over to the car and jumped in beside him.

As the car pulled out of the driveway, Cathy turned to them. "Hey, have you guys eaten breakfast yet?"

Danny read her lips and immediately shook his head from side to side.

Cathy laughed. "Rick, to the house and get started on some pancakes, pronto. Our guests look like they're starving. We'll get some food into you and then figure out who to call. Sound good, boys?"

Rick glanced at him through the rear-view mirror. "Hey, just to keep your paranoia, and mine, in check, can you guys keep your heads down while we drive through town? You're celebrities around here and you don't want to attract any additional attention until we figure out who to call, okay?"

Michael and Danny hunkered down in their seats.

Within minutes they pulled up to a small, but charming cape, set back on an acre of property and surrounded by the woods on three sides. It gave the house a safe, private feel. As soon as the Somerses took them inside, Rick locked the door and closed the curtains.

Michael stared at Rick. "And I thought I was paranoid!"

"Well, I saw on the news what they did to your house," Rick said. "That's the last thing I want to happen here, especially before I sell it."

Good point.

Rick brought them into a bright, yellow and white kitchen. Sunflowers abounded on the wallpaper, napkins, and the cheery tablecloth in front of him.

Michael sat on a plump cushion facing a beautiful bay window which opened out onto the woods. A flood of trees bloomed in front of him, reminding him of a camping trip he had taken with his dad the summer before. They had hiked for nearly five miles before they had made camp. It had been so isolated and beautiful. He would do anything to be able to do that with his dad one more time. "Why in the world are you guys looking to move?" he said. "This place is great."

Cathy smiled. "This place is great for two people, but it's a little small for three." She patted her stomach.

Michael smiled. "Congratulations. My brother loves babies. Been bugging my mother for years to have another one."

Rick spoke up. "Okay, boys, ladies, and unborn children. Who's ready for pancakes?" Immediately, three sets of hands went up and Rick set to work. Michael and Danny ate like they hadn't eaten in days, which was pretty much true.

Rick spoke over Danny's shoulder. "I'm thinking we go straight to the FBI or the CIA and forget about the local police. You're saying Herrington's agents are posing as cops, so if we went to them we wouldn't know who to believe and who not to believe. What do you think?"

Michael nodded. "Just as long as it's someone who can protect us and can help us find our parents. Thank you so much." His voice shook.

Cathy smiled and squeezed his arm. "It'll be okay, Michael. I promise. Everything will turn out okay."

After they were stuffed, Rick suggested Michael bring his brother into the den where they could watch some TV while he and Cathy cleaned up. Michael showed his brother into the family room and turned on the television to a program Danny would like. You could always depend on The Disney Channel to come through. When he got him settled, he asked Danny to stay in the den while he went to thank the Somerses for breakfast and help them clean up.

He had the nicest thoughts about them while strolling down the hall. He turned the corner, just outside the kitchen, humming a tune from one of his favorite bands, but paused when he heard the Somerses arguing. He hung back.

Rick's voice was hushed, annoyed. "Cathy, we've got to turn them in. Think of the money we'll get!"

"But those kids trust us. We'd be betraying them."

Michael was floored. He clenched his hands into fists, feeling deceived and hurt. He peeked around the corner.

Rick was holding Cathy's hands. "Honey, this is our chance to have everything we ever wanted. Those boys are our winning lottery ticket, and they're sitting right in our family room."

Angry, Cathy shook him off. "Will you keep your voice down? It's not that I'm opposed to the money, but it feels wrong. Herrington is behind this reward money, I just know it."

Rick rolled his eyes. "If we don't turn them in, then someone else will and they'll get the money. Or, if we don't help them out, these kids will be on their own and could get themselves killed. At least we'll be keeping them safe and getting rich in the meantime."

Cathy shook her head. "Rick, Herrington is dangerous. Do you remember what he did to their house?"

He threw up his hands in frustration. "Oh, come on, Cathy, he knew they weren't there. This is because the kids' parents are spies! Traitors to the United States and the kids are probably in on it, too. At the end of the day we'll actually be helping our country get rid of a bunch of dirty agents. What do you think they're going to do? Kill them?"

She sighed. "No. I don't think they'll kill Danny. He's supposedly got some sort of special ability or something. But what about Michael? He could be the one in danger."

Michael heard the smugness in Rick's voice and wanted to punch him in his face. "Michael's a big boy, Cathy. He'll be just fine. Come on, don't blow this for us."

"Okay, okay," she said. "I guess you're right. If it isn't us, then it'll be someone else. Just do me a favor. Don't make the call in here. I don't want them to hear. Go upstairs and I'll go sit with them. Deal?"

"Sure, babe. I love you." He kissed her quickly on her forehead.

Michael didn't wait to hear any more and ran silently back to the family room, seething with anger. He was so disappointed in himself. So angry at finally trusting someone and now look where it got them. At least they got to eat breakfast.

He kneeled next to Danny with a plan. "Birdman, let's play a pretend game when Cathy comes back in here," he signed. "Pretend you have to go to the bathroom and I have to take you, okay?"

Danny nodded. Thank God he loved games. One day it wouldn't be this easy.

Cathy came into the room, trying to appear calm, but Michael knew better. The way she kept playing with her hair gave it away.

"So, you boys have a good breakfast?" she asked.

Michael gave her his sweetest smile. "Oh, yeah, it was just great. We really appreciate all you've done for us." He glanced at Danny. It was show time.

Immediately, Danny grabbed himself and whimpered.

Cathy stood up, alarmed. "What's wrong with him?"

"Oh, he just has to go to the bathroom," he laughed, watching Cathy relax. She sat back down while he stood up. "Where is it?"

"Through the kitchen and in the wash room," she answered.

Michael took Danny's hand. "Would you believe I still have to go with him? He's such a baby. We'll be right back."

He watched Cathy laugh at his lies, thinking how gullible she was. Well, the Somerses weren't the only ones who could play games. He turned to her as they left the room. "Cathy, this is going to sound weird, but could you put the volume on the television up a little louder while we're in the bathroom? Danny likes to feel the vibrations from the floor."

"He can feel the vibrations from the television?" she asked, amazed. "I had no idea."

"Oh, yeah. His deafness makes him very sensitive to those sorts of things." Danny started whining and pulled on Michael's sleeve. God, he was good. They left the room and took off towards the bathroom.

Passing through the kitchen, Michael grabbed his knapsack from the back of the kitchen chair, slung it over his shoulder and grabbed Danny's jacket from where it was hanging on a wall hook. He moved into the hallway past the kitchen and saw the bathroom. As luck would have it, the back door was next to it. He turned on the water in the sink full force, hoping that both the water and the television would drown out the sounds of him unlocking the back door. He opened it, ushering Danny outside and down the steps.

Danny protested, pulling on his arm. "No go!" he signed.

Michael turned to him. They had no time to lose. "Danny, just come with me and I'll explain later." He grabbed his brother's hand and pulled him, but Danny refused to move. In fact, he sat on the steps and crossed his arms, refusing to look at him.

Michael glanced down the hall, knowing he didn't have a lot of time. Rick should be finishing up his call and there was just so much time Cathy would give them in the bathroom before she came looking for them.

He bent to his brother, forcing him to face him. Danny closed his eyes.

Michael heard footsteps echoing down the stairs, and his heart went into a panic. He grabbed Danny's face again, but he pulled away. He snatched his hands, trying to sign into them, but Danny balled his hands into fists, and started to cry. Without thinking, Michael smacked him lightly on the back of his head to get his attention, startling them both.

Danny's eyes flew open, more out of shock than pain. Michael had never hit him before.

Michael glared at him. "Get up now," he ordered.

Danny refused to move and Michael heard Rick reach the bottom step, calling for Cathy. He picked up Danny, threw him over his shoulder and bolted the steps, two at a time,

Danny kicking and fighting him the entire time. It would be a miracle if the Somerses didn't hear them.

He ran as far as he could, running blindly through the woods, before finally collapsing to the ground. His lungs were nearly bursting, but they were far enough in that he had completely lost sight of the house.

Danny sat on the ground next to him, sobbing and punching him in his chest, throwing dirt in his face. "Why did you make us leave? You hit me. I'm going to tell Mommy."

Michael angrily pushed him aside. "I told you that you had to listen to me and you acted like a big baby."

Danny started crying even harder, and Michael was so frustrated he wanted to scream right along with his brother. They never were going to get through this if Danny wouldn't do what he said. Taking a deep breath, Michael took his brother in his arms and hugged him until he calmed down.

Danny finally looked up at him.

"Look, I'm sorry I hit you, but you wouldn't listen to me and we had to get out of that house. I know you're scared and want Mom and Dad, and I do, too. Please, walk with me for a little longer. I just can't carry you anymore."

Danny stared at him for a moment, tears streaking his cheeks, and then stood. They trekked another mile through the woods. When Michael felt Danny needed another rest, he sat him down and told him everything.

"I think you're old enough to know what's going on and this way you'll understand why I did what I did back there. Can I tell you?"

Danny nodded, wiping his nose on his sleeve.

"Remember the bad men from Mr. Jacob's house and the men who took Mr. Teddy?"

Danny nodded.

"Okay, these aren't the only people who want to find us anymore. The bad men put what's called a bounty on our heads. That means, if someone, anyone, finds us and brings us to these bad people, they'll get money. Rick and Cathy seemed great, but they were going to turn us in. I had to get us away before that happened."

"Why do they want find us?" Danny asked. "What did we do?"

"We didn't do anything, Danny, but the bad men want to find you because you have a special power."

Danny raised his eyebrows. "The birds?"

Michael nodded. "Yep. They want to find you because you can talk to the birds." He still wasn't entirely convinced what that meant though.

"But Mommy can help them talk to the birds, too," Danny signed.

Michael shook his head. "No, I don't think she can. You're special because it seems only you, out of all the people in this world, can talk to the birds and the bad men want to find out how you do it. You understand?"

Danny looked at him stonily. "Are you going to hit me again?"

Michael stifled a smile. "No, Birdman. I promise. Hey, you want another piggyback? I think I have some left in me."

He put his backpack on Danny and his brother jumped up on his back. They hiked that way through the woods for a while until they came to another neighborhood. The homes were spacious, but very close together and there weren't a lot of places to hideout and not be conspicuous. Luckily for them, it seemed quiet. It was a Wednesday, so almost everyone was either at work or school.

Michael quickly ambled through a backyard and onto the street. He finally got his bearings and thought he remembered a park at the end of the development with a tennis court, pool area, and walking path through a wooded picnic area. He moved in that direction.

When they reached the park, the first place they passed was the pool. There were some vending machines and after searching his pockets for some change he found seven quarters, three dimes, and a nickel. He dropped the change into the machine and bought some pretzels and an orange soda. Michael found them a picnic table in the woods and set Danny down on it. They ate in silence as Michael watched Danny toss some of his pretzels to the birds that came close.

"Danny," he signed, waving to get his brother's attention. "Are those just birds or are they really people?"

"Of course they're people."

Michael sat there stunned as Danny tossed crumbs at the birds and signed to Michael. "See that one there, the big one with the grey feathers? That's Mr. Hamilton. And that one with the white fuzzy throat is Mrs. Kidder."

Michael watched two small birds fly over to his brother, practically sitting on his shoes and pecking at tiny flecks of food on the ground. "They're really not scared of you, are they?" he signed, shaking his head in amazement.

"Nope," Danny replied, bending down. He tossed the last of his pretzels to the two birds. "They know I won't hurt them." Two more birds flew over to him and rested at his feet. "These two little ones are Jamie and Kimmy."

Michael moved over to stand next to Danny. The birds became startled, ready to take flight, but Danny slowly put his hands together and shut his eyes. The birds relaxed.

"What happened to them?" Michael asked, his voice hushed. "If they're really dead, why are they all still here?"

Danny cocked his head and seemed to be examining the birds. "Okay," he finally smiled. "Mr. Hamilton had an operation on his heart last year. He was really old. He said the people in the hospital tried everything, but their machines didn't work. He never made it out of the operating room. Mrs. Kidder was old, too. I think she mixed up her medicines and it's why she's here." Danny then turned his back on Mrs. Kidder, so she wouldn't see what he signed to Michael. "Mrs. Kidder is hard to talk to. I think she's a little mixed up. She doesn't know what she's doing."

"Why not?" Michael asked. "Is she sick?"

Danny nodded. "I think she had what our neighbor, Mr. Keely, had. Remember? I don't know what it's called, though."

Michael thought for a moment. Suddenly, he remembered. "Oh, you mean she had Alzheimer's."

Danny nodded. "Yeah, that's what she had when she was a person, but now she still has a little bit of it in her bird body and she can't get herself to the light. She gets all confused still."

"Danny, what about the Jamie and Kimmy birds?" Michael asked.

Danny made a solemn face. "It's sad," he signed and said no more.

"C'mon, Danny, what happened to them?"

Danny sighed. "Their Mommy got into a really bad car crash yesterday. A truck ran into them when she was taking them to school."

"Oh, my God," he muttered, feeling sick. He stared at the Jamie and Kimmy birds, watching as they pecked at the last remnants of the pretzel pieces.

Michael got Danny's attention again. "Danny, but if they died and then became birds, why are they all still here? Why haven't all of them gone up to the light yet? I mean, that's Heaven, right? So, if this is all true, then once they die in their people bodies, shouldn't they just go straight there?"

Danny shrugged. "They could, but sometimes they have reasons for staying. Do you want me to ask them?"

Michael nodded. "Yes. Please."

Danny held his hands together again and closed his eyes. The birds tittered around. Danny opened his eyes and started signing. "Jamie and Kimmy don't want to go yet. They want to wait for their Mommy. She's still in the hospital, but she's really hurt. And Mr. Hamilton's just sad and wishes he were back in his people body."

"What about Mrs. Kidder?"

"Mrs. Kidder doesn't know what she wants to do. I think she's been here a long, long time. I might have to help her."

Michael stared at him wonderingly. "And you're telling me that you can send them up to the light yourself? You have the power to do that?"

Danny nodded. "Sure, but I don't have to send them all the time. Only when they get really confused or really hurt, like Mr. Jacobs."

Suddenly, a beautiful blue jay flew down to the group. Michael watched as the blue jay and the two birds Danny had called Jamie and Kimmy gathered together. Immediately, the blue jay started preening the other two birds and then, in a flash of color and wings, they flew away together. Danny laughed delightedly as they disappeared into the trees.

Danny immediately stopped laughing when he saw his brother's stricken expression.

Michael was upset, his eyes tearing. "That was their mother, wasn't it? She just died, didn't she?"

Danny ran over and took his hand. "Don't be sad, Michael. She only left her sick people body and now she's a bird. She'll take Jamie and Kimmy away so that they can start a new life."

"A new life? Do you know what kind of life they have in Heaven, Danny?"

Danny simply shrugged. "I don't know. It must be a really nice place because everyone wants to go there. Except the bad people. They just disappear."

"They just vanish? Like magic?" Michael asked.

Danny shook his head. "No, not like that. When a person dies they go right into a bird body, but if they're a bad person, then, poof, they get killed in that body." He tried to explain. "When you see a dead bird on the street, or floating in the water, or wherever, it's usually a bad person."

"But what about Mr. Jacobs? They shot him when he was a bird, so he was going to die. Does that mean he was really bad, too?"

Danny shook his head. "No, he was a good person and the mean men shot him when he was a person and then again when he was a bird. They tried to completely kill him. Mommy says I have special powers so if a good person gets hurt while he's in a bird body, I can help him get to Heaven. If I don't send him, he'll just roam the Earth until he gets R-I-N-C-I-N-A-T-E-D." He tried to fingerspell the word, but had trouble.

"I don't understand." Michael said. "Spell it again."

Danny tried again.

Michael finally understood. "Oh, you mean reincarnated. Wait a second! You mean they come back to life? How do they do that?"

"When a bird lays an egg, silly!" Danny laughed.

Michael was speechless and shook his head. "Okay, let me get this straight. You're saying good birds can always take themselves to the light when they're ready, right?"

Danny nodded.

"And, if we see a dead bird on the ground or the road or whatever, then most of the time, that was a bad person who was bad when he was a human being? So his soul simply disappears and he can't go to Heaven, right?"

Danny nodded again.

Michael was getting excited. "Okay, I think I'm getting this. So what you're saying is birds can stay on Earth as long as they like and lead bird lives until they choose to go to

Heaven? And when a bird lays an egg, that's a good person who died when he was a bird before he got the chance to go to heaven?"

Danny clapped his hands and nodded yes.

I think I'm finally getting it.

Danny added more. "You want to know something else? Eggs can also be little, little babies. A lot of times when people babies die they never get a chance to have a people life and so they get to be the baby birds."

"Unbelievable," Michael said, looking around. The trees were brimming with the sounds of birds, and he knew he'd never be able to look at them the same way again.

Danny was trying to get his attention. "Remember when my friend Cindy's daddy died?"

Michael nodded.

"Cindy's mommy got her a bird to keep her company."

Michael couldn't believe it. "That was her dad? No way."

Danny nodded. "Cindy cried and cried when the bird flew away a few months later, but her Daddy just wanted to stay with her until he knew she'd be okay. I tried to tell her that he was fine, but she didn't believe me. Do you understand?"

Michael did. As he sat there thinking about it, he remembered something. "Hey, Danny, what about the machine? What is it?"

Danny shrugged. "Mommy calls it ultraviolet. She says the colors inside help me to talk to the birds. I tried to tell her that I talked to the birds all the time without the light, but she says it will help me focus. She said when I was a baby in her tummy the ultraviolet accident made me deaf so I could hear the birds. So I could have special powers."

At least Dobber hadn't lied about everything.

A sound made him turn and Michael watched the Mrs. Kidder bird flapping her wings and tittering around in circles. He got up to take a closer look and saw she had gotten both her legs caught up in the plastic wrapper of a six-pack someone had thoughtlessly left lying on the ground. Michael moved to try to help her, but she became scared and skittish and kept trying to fly away. The wrapper got even more tangled around her thin legs.

As Michael tried in vain to help the bird, he felt a light tap on his back. Danny was signing to him. "It's time, Michael. She has to go away. She can't do it by herself."

Danny turned to the bird, clasped his hands together and shut his eyes.

Mrs. Kidder stiffened and faced Danny. All her skittishness and fright disappeared. Danny bent over her and picked her up, gently cradling her in his hands. Just like the last time, Michael saw an instantaneous beam of white light shoot up out of his hands and encircle the bird. Immediately, the bird became lax in his brother's hands while he glanced up into the sky, smiling. The faintest of shadows seemed to streak across the sky.

Slowly, Danny moved over to a nearby tree and gently laid Mrs. Kidder beneath some undergrowth. Then he turned back to Michael who stared at him.

"Danny, did you just kill her?"

"I didn't kill her," he said, indignantly. "She wanted to go to the light, and she was so sick she would never be able to find it by herself. That's why she's been here so long. I just helped her like Mommy and Daddy showed me."

Michael was thunderstruck. He now realized what this power truly meant. His brother was playing God. His family had never been particularly religious, only going to church on Holy Days, but Danny's actions struck him to the core. If a human's soul left its body when it died and was transferred to a bird, then it could be considered alive at that point. Was Danny justified in sending them on to the light by killing them? Is that what Herrington wanted? To control the birds and thus, the people in the world? He pictured humongous pens for millions and millions of birds with the members of Herrington's organization deciding who would and who would not get the chance to go to Heaven. Or, which bird he'd kill outright if someone's family didn't pay up and that person's soul would be gone forever.

He had a disturbing thought and turned to his brother. "Danny, what about chickens and turkeys or all those birds we eat for dinner? Are they people, too?" He was horrified to think he might be personally responsible for sending people to their untimely deaths and stopping them from going to Heaven.

Danny made a face at him. "No. We eat chickens, silly. Only pretty birds that can fly up into the sky are people."

"Like bluebirds and doves and stuff like that?"

"Yes," Danny explained. "And pet birds and even eagles. But, not chickens or turkeys or big birds like ostriches. They can't fly more than a few feet. They could never get high enough to go to the light."

Michael sat back. "Unbelievable."

They stayed in the park for the next few hours. He was sure the Somerses had made the call to Herrington's people, but they were now miles away from their house and he felt secure for the moment. By three o'clock, he knew they had to leave. Kids were getting off from school, and the park was starting to fill up. He and Danny made their way out of the park and the moment they came to the entrance to the main road, two brown sedans came whizzing around the corner.

Chapter Eight

Day 3 Wednesday 3:02 p.m.

Michael moved behind a group of trees and peeked around a tree trunk. The sedans were idling and several uniformed policemen showed passers-by photographs. They looked like fakes to Michael and he couldn't imagine why people didn't just cringe from being too close to them. As for who were in the photographs? Well, he didn't have to think too hard about the subject of the pictures. Person after person shook his head until an old man, who Michael had seen sitting on a park bench near them for most of the afternoon, nodded. The man stared at the picture for a long time and then slowly pointed in their direction.

"Why's he pointing at us?" Danny signed.

"Because the men who are after us are here. We've got to go." He backed away and quickly led Danny deeper into the park.

"Where are we going to go?" Danny asked.

"I've got an idea."

Michael took them around the outside of the park and they exited on the east side which led to an area with a small local hospital, a library, and a post office. After weighing his options, Michael turned towards the hospital. The library had too many kids and the post office was closing at four.

Michael went through the main doors and straight into the gift shop.

"Can I help you, boys?" an elderly woman manning the register asked. She smiled, her face cascading into a mound of wrinkles.

He couldn't help smiling back. "Yes, ma'am. Would you know if the cafeteria is still open?"

"Oh, I think they closed at three," she said. After looking at Danny's crestfallen face, she called Michael over to her.

"I've got a better idea than the cafeteria, and it won't cost you anything either, dear." She handed him a hall pass from her front sweater pocket.

"On the ninth floor, outside the Geriatric Ward, they're giving out snacks to the residents and their families. It's a special floor. Would you believe a hotel runs it?"

Michael knew about those private floors. A friend's dad from his history class had surgery a few years before and he had stayed at Harlem River Hospital in Manhattan. The kid had come back telling them about how the entire floor looked like a hotel and there was actually a concierge who would direct people to their relative's rooms.

Michael gratefully took the pass. "You don't think they'll give us a problem?"

The woman smiled. "Oh no, you should be just fine. If anyone questions you, just flash the pass. I'm sure no one will even say anything, but if they do, tell them I sent you."

"This is great. Thank you so much. We really appreciate it." He led Danny over to the elevators. Michael flashed the pass at the security guard and sighed in relief when the guard waved them in.

As the doors opened on nine, Michael searched for the signs to the Geriatric Ward. He finally found them and moved through the double doors into a different world.

The first thing he noticed was the smell. The antiseptic hospital aroma was gone, replaced with the perfume of hundreds of flowers. They were displayed in vases on every available open space. Ahead, in a carpeted atrium, snacks were set out on a white linen tablecloth with real dishes and silverware. A man in a tuxedo was playing classical music on a grand piano, accompanied by a lone violinist. Visitors and patients milled about as if they were at a garden party instead of a hospital floor.

Taking a deep breath, and hoping desperately they would simply blend in and not be recognized, Michael walked Danny over to the snack table. He made them each a plate of tuna fish finger sandwiches and chocolate chip cookies. He was relieved no one questioned him. Michael turned to give Danny his plate and saw he wasn't next to him. Fear flooded his body. His adrenaline racing, he dropped their plates on the table and frantically searched around, finally noticing his brother on the far side of the room, sitting on a striped upholstered couch next to an old man connected to a portable IV drip. The man was holding Danny's hands.

Michael quickly walked over to them, not knowing if he wanted to yell at Danny for leaving his side without telling him, or to hug him until he squirmed.

He was saved either choice by the old man. "This your little brother?" he asked, his voice hoarse.

Michael nodded.

The man patted Danny's head. "He's a good little boy. I can feel it. I don't have much family left, and it's nice to hold a little one close every now and then. I don't know how much time I have left to do this." He sadly released Danny's hands. "Seeing little ones always reminds me of how precious life is."

Danny turned to Michael. "Tell him he's going to be okay. He's not ready to go to the light yet. The medicines the doctors are giving him are working." Michael stalled and Danny pulled on his sleeve. "It's true, Michael, tell him. He needs to know so he'll fight harder!"

Watching the man's labored breathing, Michael felt he might be giving him false hope, but Danny kept tugging on his sleeve. He turned to the man. "Sir, my brother feels you have more time than you think. That the medicines you're taking are working." How in the world could Danny know this? Whatever power he had, he wasn't a doctor.

"Well, we'll just have to hope he's right, won't we?" the man sighed. "Time will tell. It always does, one way or another." The man stood and moved over to the snack table, dragging his IV unit behind him.

After retrieving their food, Michael brought Danny over to a patio table to eat. "How can you possibly know that man will be okay?" Michael asked, before stuffing a tiny sandwich into his mouth.

"It's easy. There aren't any birds waiting around for him."

Michael was about to pop another sandwich in his mouth but stopped, mid-bite. "What?"

Danny looked at him as if he were the dumbest brother on the planet. "If that man was going to die, there'd be a bird waiting for him. And I don't see any birds here. At least, not any waiting for him."

Michael whirled around. "Where do you see birds? I don't see any."

Danny pointed towards the window. "There's some out there. Can't you see them?"

He looked to where Danny was pointing. A few were outside on the window ledge, pecking at flecks of food.

"Oh, yeah, I can see them," Michael said, confused. "But I thought all birds were people. Are you telling me some birds don't have any souls yet? That they just wait around for someone to die?"

"Kind of. Mommy said when a person is a bird and finally goes to the light the bird body has to go somewhere so it's empty until it gets called," Danny explained.

"You mean like an empty vessel?" Michael asked. "How can that be? Who controls them?"

"There are things Mommy says she doesn't know, but she read about angels and she's sure that when someone leaves a bird body and goes to the light, an angel takes over the bird until someone else is called."

"And you can tell when a bird has no soul inside?"

Danny nodded. "Those birds on the windowsill outside have no souls inside them yet, but I can tell who they're waiting for."

Michael leaned closer to Danny and glanced around, grimacing. "Are they for anyone around here?"

"Not for anyone having snacks. They're waiting for some of the people in the rooms."

Michael was creeped out. "Danny, how can you possibly know this?"

Danny shrugged. "I just do. They talk to me and tell me. Just like those birds in the park. It's like a picture of what they want to tell me comes into my mind and I can understand what they're saying. You understand?"

Michael shook his head. "I'm trying, Danny. I'm really trying. So those birds outside can talk to you. What are they saying?"

"They're not talking to me now, but they know I know what they are."

Michael rubbed his shoulders, chilled. "It's just all so unbelievable." He stood. "You want some more food?"

Danny nodded. After they ate for a little while longer, Michael glanced at his watch. He wanted it to be later so he and Danny could move around easier. That's when he decided he would call the FBI himself. He tapped his brother lightly on the shoulder to get his attention.

"Those fake cops should be gone by now but I want us to get going. I saw the buses come on the hour and it's about four. Hey, I've got a great idea. Want to go catch a movie?" That would buy them a few more hours. Sitting in a dark theater had to be safer than walking around the streets.

Danny jumped up and down excitedly.

They returned the hall pass and made their way outside, walking over to the bus stop. Two minutes later the M6 came to take them through the heart of town near the mall, where there was a ten-plex theater.

The driver broke a five-dollar bill and within seconds, he and Danny were hunkered down in the backseat of the bus. Michael sat back and relaxed as he watched his brother stare out the window.

Twenty-five minutes later, the bus let them off near the movie theater and Michael purchased two tickets for the showing of the latest Disney movie at five. They were a little early, so the theater was still relatively empty and no one gave them a second glance. They made themselves comfortable up front. Since he couldn't hear the film, Danny always liked to sit as close as possible to the screen. He said it made him feel like he was really in the movie.

Two and a half hours later, after seven promos and a feature-length film, the movie ended and the lights came on. Danny jumped up.

"Hey, Danny," Michael said, pulling him back. "Stay in your seat until everyone leaves. I don't want us to attract any attention."

It was too late.

"Hey, Mommy! That kid signed to that little boy. He looks like the one from TV."

Michael turned to see a small child pointing in their direction and his stomach somersaulted. Ten seconds ago they had been anonymous. Now the entire theater stared at them. Some of the adults actually screamed and pulled their children back into their seats as if Michael and Danny had the plague. The rest of the people glared at them threateningly, and some of the men started to move towards them. Michael stood and took his brother's hand.

"You're making a mistake," he said. "We're not those kids on TV."

"Oh, really?" an angry, bearded guy asked, as he made is way down the aisle. "That's funny, because you sure look like them, you little murderer. Now, why don't you stay right there, keep your hands where we can see them, and hopefully no one else will get hurt."

Murderer? "What are you talking about? I didn't kill anyone."

The man kept advancing and Michael started to back up. He turned, seeing a neon exit sign at the front of the theater.

"Listen, you stay away from us," Michael yelled. "I'm telling you, you're making a mistake." Out of the corner of his eye he could see a second man slinking quickly through the aisles, trying to cut them off from the side.

"Watch out, he might have a gun or a bomb," someone yelled. Screams tore through the theater as mothers flooded the aisles with their children, desperate to flee the room.

Michael saw the looks in everyone's eyes, the anger, the fear, and knew none of these people would help them. He signed to his brother, lightning fast. "Run to the exit behind me. The bad men are here." Danny immediately turned and ran. Michael was close behind him. He flung open the doors and heard them swing shut, drowning out the noise of the other men running full speed down the aisles after them.

"Danny, run that way!" Michael signed, once they were outside. "Through the cars." It was crowded in the parking lot, and he hoped they'd be able to lose themselves in all the vehicles.

As they sprinted through the lot they attracted more and more attention. There were shrieks and screams. "Look! It's them. The kids from TV. Get them!" Michael was never so angry and scared in his entire life. He didn't know why everyone was turning on him and his brother. They were just kids. It didn't make sense. Did they actually think he had killed someone?

Understanding flooded him. Mr. Jacobs. He was being framed. There was a bounty on their heads and people weren't just going to help Herrington's people find them because their parents might have worked for Herrington. They were going to turn them in because they were considered killers. He wanted to throw up.

They plunged out of the parking lot and behind an Applebee's restaurant.

Danny whimpered. "I'm scared."

"I know, but we can't stop yet or we won't get away. Look, over there is another motel." He pointed towards a Days Inn situated behind the restaurant. They ran toward the motel and through the main lobby and out to the inner courtyard. A few patrons jumped out of the way as they raced past them. When they got to the courtyard, Michael pulled

Danny upstairs. "Come on. I need to get a better look at who's after us."

Peeking around the corner of the second floor of the motel, he saw about fifteen people milling around the dumpster of the Applebee's. He could see them scanning the area and a few of them were yelling.

Michael grabbed Danny, pulling him down the hallway towards the back parking lot of the motel. It was backed against a cemetery. They bolted down the steps and across the lot. Michael hoisted Danny over a small rock wall enclosing the cemetery and together they started running, trying to lose the crowd for the moment.

The cemetery was empty and after a few minutes Michael felt a little safer and sat Danny on a concrete bench. He knew it was only a matter of time before their luck ran out. Someone was going to catch them. Danny started to tremble. Michael leaned over and put his arms around him to comfort him. It wasn't much, but his brother calmed down a little. Now he knew how escaped convicts felt.

A cool breeze brushed by them, and Danny shivered. Michael leaned over and zipped up the nylon windbreaker Danny had put on that morning. He wished he had his own jacket. The breeze brought more than just cold air. It also brought voices, and through the rustling of the trees, Michael heard the sound of angry people. They were far away but he knew it was the men and women from the theater. Worse, it sounded like their numbers had grown in size. No matter how many there were, Michael would fight every last one of them to keep his brother safe. He had seen first-hand how crazy people could get when they wanted something really bad, be it a fight over a girlfriend or the latest hot toy during the holidays. People became insane. He could just imagine three or four men each trying to make a grab for Danny. They would tear him apart. The worst part was, they wouldn't even care. Danny was no longer a person—not even a little kid in their minds. They had both become nothings.

Michael stood. "Danny, we have to go. Come on."

They made their way briskly through the cemetery. The area was well lit, but there were plenty of dark patches to stay in. After a few minutes they reached a small mausoleum and from their vantage point, could see the front gates.

"I don't want to go through the front entrance," Michael signed to Danny. "The people might be waiting for us." No sooner had he said that when he saw the sedans pull up outside the gates. Even Danny recognized them for what they were and cringed, pushing up against his brother for protection.

"Baa mem," Danny said, trying to speak.

"Yeah, that's right, Birdman, bad men," Michael echoed.

He led Danny across the main reception building and over to a rock wall on the far side of the cemetery. This one was harder to climb, and Michael had to actually piggyback

Danny over it as they made their escape. As they jumped down to the other side, Michael saw they were in someone's back yard. He put his brother down, and they ran through the yard to the front of the house.

All of a sudden he heard the shout he was hoping not to hear. "I see them. There they are."

Michael desperately searched for the source of the voice, but it was too dark. Then, he finally saw the crowd. It was so much bigger than he had thought, and he became paralyzed with fear. There were approximately thirty people running towards them from the end of the long block. Michael tried to move, but he couldn't, his limbs were frozen.

It was Danny who came through. He started screaming, jerking Michael back to reality with a sick thud. Danny never screamed like that and the sound chilled Michael's heart. His paralysis broke.

He pushed Danny and they ran blindly through the neighborhood, trying desperately to lose the crowd. Michael suddenly found his bearings and pulled Danny through a side street into a backyard. Through the trees Michael could see the outline of Rockland County High School. They sprinted across the street.

The side door by the gym was open for practices that night. He raced with his brother towards the entrance and into the school. What he needed was a weapon and remembered the dissecting knives in the biology lab. They bolted upstairs to the lab and burst in on Mr. Daley, Michael's high school biology teacher. One look at them and Daley took control.

Day 4 Thursday 5:00 a.m.

In the car.

Michael took another long look at his sleeping brother and turned back to the road. After a few more hours of driving, Michael pulled the car into a truck stop and parked in the rear where he hoped no one would bother them. It was now daylight, but he just couldn't drive anymore. He desperately needed some sleep. Danny had woken up, but was now content to play with some paper and pencils he had found in the back seat of Daley's car.

"Danny, I need to take a nap for a little while," he explained. "Wake me if anyone comes near the car, okay?"

Danny nodded and started drawing.

Michael woke up almost three hours later to Danny pulling on his leg.

Sheepishly, he signed, "I have to go to the bathroom."

Michael rubbed his eyes, groggy. "It's time for us to get something to eat anyway, and I have to fill up the car with gas." He opened the car door and the both of them took care of business in a crop of bushes.

They zipped up, and Michael nodded. "Okay, let's go."

Chapter Nine

Day 4, After a full day of driving: 8:00 p.m.

"Wait here," Michael signed. He got up to answer the door. "Who's there?"

"Room service," a man's voice answered.

"Just a second." He waved at Danny to hide in the bathroom. Michael released the deadbolt, removed the chain on the door, and let the steward inside, keeping his head down and trying to hide his face behind his hair.

"Where do you want it?"

"On the bed is fine," Michael answered.

After the steward put down the tray, Michael sifted a five-dollar bill from his pocket. "Thanks," he said.

The steward took the bill and left the room.

Michael relocked the door and turned to get Danny. He couldn't help laughing. His brother was peering around the corner of the wall. All Michael could see was the very top of his head and his big brown eyes. "It's okay to come out now, you geek. Come on, let's chow down, my man."

They dove into the hamburgers and fries. As an extra treat he had ordered them both hot fudge sundaes for dessert. They were half-melted by the time they got to them, but they were still great, making them feel some semblance of the comforts of home.

"Are we going to stay here?" Danny asked, ice cream dribbling down his chin and onto the comforter. "I like this place much better than the other hotel."

"We can't stay, Birdman," he said. "We've got to find the man Mr. Daley told us about. He's going to be able to help us get out of this. Besides, Mr. Daley gave us some money, and I don't want to blow it all on hotels."

Back in Rockland County, and then once in Pennsylvania, Michael used his credit card to fill up the gas tank and stock the car with bottled water and snack food and then threw it out into a garbage can at one of the rest stops. If anything, all those spy movies he had watched were finally coming in handy. In every single one of them, someone always got nailed because the bad guys traced the person by his credit card. They would only be able to trace him so far.

After dinner, Michael could see that Danny was fading fast. He removed the tray and tucked him into one side of the king-size bed. "Don't you worry about a thing, Birdman. We're on our way to people who can help us." Michael trusted Daley. He had always liked the teacher and he had an air about him that made you feel like he really cared about you. Michael kissed his brother on the cheek.

"Goodnight, Michael," Danny signed and closed his eyes.

Michael shut the lights off and turned on the television. He had to find out what people were saying about them. What he heard horrified him. Apparently, he was being blamed for the death of Scout Master Mark Jacobs and also for the death of the 7-Eleven clerk. The word on the street was he was a traitor along with his parents.

The newscaster spoke to the audience. "Please be advised Michael is considered armed and dangerous. Hi-Core Industries is devastated at the connection to their company and has offered a five million dollar reward for finding the boys."

A picture of Mr. Jacobs surrounded by a team of Boy Scouts flashed on the screen, another with the clerk holding a guitar and singing with a band onstage. Michael thought he was going to be sick.

Now, an old video of Michael when he was in a play in junior high popped up on the screen, along with some recent photographs of him in the chess club and the varsity swim team. His dinner gurgled in his stomach. It was disconcerting to watch his younger self, parading as a pirate in Peter Pan for the world to see. He couldn't believe how much his life had changed in just days. How out of control it had become. The things they were accusing him of. Someone had to know the truth. He had to get to California, to the man Daley was sending him to. He had to be the one to help them.

Disgusted, he shut off the television, but not before a photo of his entire family from a fishing trip they took last summer flashed on the screen. Seeing his parents made his stomach lurch. He hoped it wasn't the last picture they had all taken together.

He lay on the bed and spoke to the shadows. "Mom, Dad, where are you? I don't know what you did and I don't care anymore if you're spies or not. I need you."

Michael turned to his side and fell into a troubled sleep.

Chapter Ten

Day 2, Tuesday afternoon

The van was bouncing wildly, and Madeline Anderson was scared beyond reason. Kidnapped at gunpoint and learning Herrington had found out what they had done was the worst-case scenario she had been briefed on. To be attacked in such a public venue was nothing she had been prepared for. The assailants had been rough with them, and she could feel stickiness on her face where the butt of a gun had hit her temple. She tried to move her hands, but the ropes were so tight her fingers had become numb. She couldn't see or speak because of the blindfold and gag and had no way to call out to Gary.

The vehicle came to a sudden halt and she was herded out, grabbed by her hair and pushed across a hard surface. She heard the faraway sounds of small engines, wondering if they were at an airport. When they moved her up a flight of stairs and bound her into a chair, she knew at once where they were going. Somewhere far. To a place where Herrington could talk to them. She knew his ways and knew what that meant. He was nothing unless he had a syringe with some excruciating liquid in his hands as his weapon.

They flew for hours. Someone untied her once for a bathroom break and some water, but they kept her blindfold on so she couldn't see Gary. She figured they were on their way to California to Herrington's home base. That was where Marta was. It was all the man thought about these days. Served him right. It was one of his own diseases which had gotten her sick.

Maddy remembered meeting Marta while she and Gary were training with Herrington. She was a small spit of a girl with a coldness about her, which made Maddy wince when she came near, as if she'd get frostbite if she touched her. Rumors abounded about the crimes Marta committed before she worked for Herrington, but the man adored her and would do anything for her. And had.

She and Gary had lived on a few different islands while they trained. Michael had been born on a private island near Vanuatu, where Herrington housed one of his larger laboratories, and she and Gary had begun their research on light therapy there, always with the concentration and side experiments on the afterlife happening in the background. Michael had been so confused when they finally returned to the States, wanting to know why there wasn't an ocean in his backyard. It was one of the reasons they'd built the pool.

Maddy steeled herself for how bad things could get. She felt the plane land and when the door opened she was pulled roughly to her feet and down the staircase, into a vehicle, and thrown like garbage onto the floor, which she assumed was a van as there was enough room for her to lie down. Someone was thrown next to her, their bodies pressed together and she knew it was Gary. She just contented herself to lie next to him until they got to their destination.

The vehicle drove for another lengthy amount of time, before doors opened and she was ushered into a building and down a hall, the tile floor cold on her bare feet. A door opened and again she was thrown onto the floor. She heard another person drop to the ground next to her and then the doors slammed shut. She rolled herself over to the stranger till she bumped into him, feeling her husband and simply lay next to him, waiting. She smelled the salt of the ocean, and knew they were close to Herrington. All his labs were near the ocean. It was only a matter of time before she found out what he was going to do with them.

Chapter Eleven

Three days later…

Maddy closed her eyes and felt her body quickly slipping away. Herrington stormed into the room and shook her savagely, causing her to scream in agony as he yanked her chained wrists. "Get up, Maddy. There's no sleep for you until you answer my questions." He turned to his interrogator, a huge, dark imposing man towering over six and a half feet tall.

The interrogator leaned in. "I'll give you another chance to answer the question, Madeline. Where's the boy? We know you had a tracking device on him, but the signal is no longer responding. Who do you have on the inside working with you? Who removed it?"

"I keep telling you. I don't know where he is or how to find him. And no one is working with us," she cried.

Herrington smiled, and it was pure evil. He nodded his head in Gary's direction and Maddy cringed, her chest tightening so much she could barely breathe. They had been abusing Gary for the past three days, beating him, hoping if they tortured her husband, she'd finally give them the information they needed, but what he wanted was Danny and she and Gary were both prepared to die rather than hand over their son to this monster.

She stared at her husband, now passed out on the floor, but they were going to revive him again soon. The smelling salts were stacked like children's blocks next to him.

She had to continue the charade at all costs. Still, it wasn't much of a charade. She really didn't know where Michael and Danny were. And now the tracking device in Danny's ear was, for some reason, not working. She was thankful for that. It meant, for the moment, they were safe.

"So, you still don't want to talk?" The interrogator turned to Herrington and the man nodded, taking a syringe from an aide behind him. "Do it."

Despite herself, Maddy started screaming, terrified of what was in that syringe. "Mr. Herrington, please, I don't know where they are. I'm sorry for what we did, but please, spare my husband. He was only trying to protect the boys and me. I'll tell you anything else, how Danny gets his powers, what the light is, what he can do. Just please don't hurt Gary anymore," she begged.

Herrington ignored her pleas and handed the needle to the interrogator who walked over to Gary and plunged it into his arm. Gary woke up, screaming. Maddy started shrieking as loudly as Gary as she watched him writhing in pain, welts and boils erupting all over his body.

They had been on the road for almost five hours. Michael had pulled over to buy a map, trying to avoid the most populated areas while they drove across the country. He would have loved this if they weren't running for their lives.

They didn't stop that evening until Michael thought he was going to drop. He saw a sign for a twenty-five dollar per night room rate at a small roadside motel, so he decided to splurge and checked them in, rather than sleep in the car for the night. Though the beds were a bit hard and the room had a musty smell, they both fell asleep quickly.

At three in the morning, Michael awoke to Danny crying in his sleep. He yelled, "Day, Day," over and over again.

His call for Father.

Michael shook his brother awake and tried to calm him, telling him he was just having a nightmare.

Danny trembled uncontrollably and kept glancing at the window.

"Danny, what is it?" When Danny didn't respond to him he took his brother's chin in his hand and forced him to face him. "Everything is okay, you just had a bad dream. I'm here. Everything is okay."

Danny shook his head no. "It was Daddy," he signed, crying. "The birds are coming for him."

"No, Daddy's fine. You just had a bad dream."

Danny shook his head forcibly. "It wasn't a dream. The birds are coming, and they're coming here!"

Michael rose to open the shades to show Danny nothing was there. "Trust me. It was just a nightmare, but I'll check anyway. Look, see? No birds."

Michael shrieked and jumped back when he saw an enormous bird crouching right outside the window, and staring directly at him. It was a California Condor, the one bird he had spent a long time talking to his father about.

Could it be? "Dad?" Michael asked hesitantly, taking a tentative step towards the window. He blinked once and, suddenly, the bird disappeared.

Michael turned back at his brother who was crying uncontrollably. "See, I told you. It was Daddy. They're hurting him."

"Oh, my God," Michael said, running over to his brother and holding his shaking body. He tried to speak, but couldn't think of anything to say, terrified of what was happening to his Dad. He glanced at the window again, but the condor was gone.

Day 6 Saturday 2:00 p.m.

Maddy screamed. "Stop, you're killing him! Please!"

The guards ignored her and whipped her husband for the fourth time.

"Please," she said, tears streaming down her face. "I'll tell you anything if you'll stop hurting him."

The interrogator raised his hand to the guard to stop the lashing and stared at Herrington, who stood silently in the corner, tapping the wall with his jeweled fingers. Herrington squinted at her. "You're hardly in a position to bargain." He stormed over to Gary and grabbed the back of his head, yanking it up so Maddy could see his face. She screamed in anguish when she saw the welts across his cheeks, the whip marks down his bare chest.

"Was it worth it to you? Did you think you could deceive me and never be found out? Now, unless you tell me what I want to know, you'll be next," he said, releasing Gary to his tortured misery, where he had passed out again. He then grabbed her face in his hands. "We wouldn't want to ruin that pretty face of yours, too, would we?" He threw her to the floor. "Now tell me again about the accident and how Danny came to have his powers."

"I t-t-told you this already," she stuttered, between sobs. "I was working on a light therapy technique with ultraviolet rays and something went wrong. The circuits overloaded, and I was knocked unconscious. I was pregnant with Danny at the time and he must have been affected. I'm telling you the truth. You must believe me."

He bent to her level and screeched into her face, spittle flying from his mouth. "If that's the truth then why didn't you or your husband report your theories to my men? Why didn't you tell me your son could communicate with the dead? That

125

was your mission. Why did you send falsified documents to me and create your own machine to escalate your son's powers?" His eyes widened in comprehension. "Are you working for the United States government now? Of course you are."

"No, no, we're not," she cried. "I swear. If we were, they would have come after you years ago. We have enough information to have you locked up for your entire lifetime. I could have told them what you were doing, how many countries you're holding hostage with your bio-agents. I never did that. We were just trying to protect our son. We still weren't sure of his powers, and we didn't want to turn over our findings until we knew everything. We didn't want you to take him away from us. That's the truth."

Herrington smirked. "Touching, but I think you're lying. It was your duty to tell me everything, not just what you felt was important."

"Mr. Herrington. I can help you with Marta. I can tell you how to save her soul."

Herrington backhanded her and Maddy went flying into the wall behind her. "Don't you ever speak of Marta in my presence again. Ever."

Blood gushing from a new head wound, Maddy glared at him, undaunted. "You were going to use my son to control people. To control their fates. You aren't God."

Herrington glared at her, breathing hard. "Maybe not, but I'm close," he whispered. He turned to leave the room, and then turned back. "You and Gary made a terrible mistake, one you'll pay for with your lives at the end of this. You could have been the greatest of leaders in my emerging order, the King and Queen of the Light, so to speak. Instead, you'll be dead and I'll have your boys."

"Please, leave my children alone. You can try to recreate the accident. I'll help you. You don't need my children."

"Oh, but you're wrong. I do need them. I've already tried to recreate the experiment, and it hasn't worked. After an intense amount of testing, I'll be able to find out what genetic characteristics are in your children. Who knows, maybe the power is in Michael, too, and he just doesn't know it. Until we find them, you'll stay here. Your house is gone, your children are gone, and as far as the United States is concerned, Madeline and Gary Anderson are traitors who sold themselves out for money. Their children are involved in the deaths of two innocent civilians and a five million dollar bounty has been put on their heads. Trust me, Maddy, they won't be missing for very long." He turned to leave the room.

"Oh, by the way," he said, tossing an object from outside into the room. "I thought you might want to have this." The object landed at Maddy's feet. She screamed at Herrington as he laughed and slammed the door shut behind him.

The man had thrown Mr. Teddy at her feet.

Chapter Twelve

Day 6 Saturday 9:15 p.m.

"Danny, we've got trouble." The car inched slowly ahead toward the police roadblock. Flashing red strobe lights illuminated the interior of the car. They had been driving all day and Michael had wanted to get in as much mileage as possible before they stopped for the night. They were now somewhere outside of California, so close...

"Hunker down and pretend you're sleeping."

Danny immediately closed his eyes.

Michael had a very bad feeling about this. He looked all of his seventeen years and since he only had his learner's permit, he legally wasn't allowed to drive this late outside of the New York tri-state area.

He saw the car in front of him get waved along and there was no way he could turn around without being noticed.

Michael slowly approached the policeman who shined a flashlight into the car.

"What can I do for you, Officer?" he asked, rolling down his window.

"Just routine checking," he replied, scanning the flashlight through the car. "Who's the kid?"

"My brother. He fell asleep a little while ago. We're on our way home from a family party. Is there something going on I should know about?"

The officer ignored the question and instead took a whistle out of his pocket and blew on it. Loudly. The sound that screeched throughout the car was deafening, and Michael involuntarily put his hands to his ears. Danny, on the other hand, never stirred.

"Your brother's a sound sleeper," the officer said, wryly.

Michael didn't like his tone.

The policeman shined the light directly into Michael's face and Michael knew exactly what was going on. Even here in the middle of nowhere, they were looking for them. His mind raced with indecision. Did he hit the gas and hope to outrun the police? That wasn't likely. There was another cop car right up ahead and a line of cars behind him. He was trapped.

The cop put his hand out. "Can I see some I.D.?"

"Why? I haven't done anything wrong."

The cop leaned into the car, his hands on the door. "Your I.D., kid. Right now. I have an idea you shouldn't be driving around here this late at night."

Michael took out his driver's license and resignedly handed it to the officer.

The officer took one look at it and turned to Michael. "Out of the car, now."

He didn't move.

The cop pointed a finger in his face. "When an officer says to get out of your car, you do it. Move."

Michael opened his door and got out. Once outside, it went down fast. The officer grabbed him and threw him against the hood of the car, yelling at the other officers that he found them.

Suddenly, four policemen joined them. Two of them held Michael while two others yanked open the passenger side door and grabbed Danny. Immediately, Danny started to scream, but they ignored his cries and carried him over to a police cruiser parked on the side of the road. They put him inside and slammed the door.

Michael frantically tried to fight the cops, tried to break free. "Where are you taking my brother?"

"Calm down, kid, or I'll TASER you, you hear? Don't worry about your brother. He's going to be just fine. Now, let's go." One of the officers grabbed Michael and brought him over to another car. Within seconds, he was inside and was being driven off into the night.

Michael pressed his face against the bulletproof glass, pounding the officers with questions. "Where are you taking me? Why are you doing this? You're cops. You're supposed to be the good guys."

The officer in the passenger seat turned on him haughtily. "Hey, Joe, our little killer is confused. He doesn't understand what's happening to him. That's just so sad, I could cry." He pretended he was sobbing.

"I'm not a killer," Michael yelled. "You're making a mistake. I demand you tell me where you're taking me."

The officer whirled around and rammed his gun against the glass, causing Michael to jump back in fear. "You're in no position to demand anything. The best thing you can do for yourself and your freak brother is not ask questions, but answer them. Maybe you'd care to start by telling us how he talks to dead people?"

"I'm not going to tell you anything." He leaned back against the seat and folded his arms across his chest stubbornly.

"Hell, you don't want to talk, fine with us," Joe said. "It doesn't matter what you say, neither of us will believe you anyway." With that the officers faced forward and said no more for the next twenty minutes.

They pulled up to a drab gray police station in the middle of the woods. It looked like a small courthouse, and they handcuffed Michael and ushered him inside. As he was hustled up the steps he was relieved to see the other officers taking Danny out of the back seat of the other police car. Michael could tell he had been crying, and his heart broke. Danny saw Michael and started to sob hysterically.

"Can I please go to my brother? He's just a little kid, and he's frightened."

"Don't worry. You'll see him in a minute." Joe brought Michael into the building and directed him down a long hallway and through a door marked Containment Area Ahead. Once inside the room, the hallway broke into three separate directions, left, right, and a staircase which led upstairs. The officer went up the steps and took Michael into a long room full of empty jail cells. He pushed him over to one on the left, unlocked his handcuffs, and shoved him inside.

As the officer relocked the steel door, Michael ran up to the bars. "Please just answer this for me—why are you doing this? We're just kids."

Joe glared at him. "Yeah, right. Just kids. Kids who killed an innocent man, a clerk at a 7-Eleven, and started a fire at their own high school, which totaled nearly fifty thousand in damage."

"I didn't do any of that, and how could you think my brother could even be involved? It was Samuel Herrington. He's the one behind all of this. His men have been chasing us all over the country. I'm telling you, I'm being framed."

Joe shook his head. "Highly unlikely. Your parent's company, Hi-Core Industries, has been working with our authorities the entire time. Told us all about your folks, how they were always difficult employees. Never filing all their studies with the company, always taking off for days and weeks at a time. They found out they've been stealing private, secure information and moving it out of the lab and they discovered where it's been going and I can tell you, it's not to Herrington. Unless the guy is a genius covering his tracks, it's another group entirely your folks are probably working with and don't think for a moment someone isn't looking into connections in Europe or the Middle East.

"Hi-Core has put a bounty on your head and you're going to be turned over to their agents and my department will be millions richer. Rich enough to take care of the wife and three kids of that Scout Master you offed in your hometown."

Michael beat at the bars. "They're lying to you—to everyone. These are the same people who took my parents— who blew up my house. Please, you have to get us to the FBI, the CIA, someone. You can't just turn us in for the money."

"Oh, I can't?" the officer spit out. "I think I very well can. So do us all a favor, kid, and stop pretending. The feigning innocence act isn't working. We both know who and what you are and this complaining is just making you look stupid. You're a spy just like your parents, and now a murderer, too."

There was a jingling of keys and a door opened. Another cop brought Danny into the containment area. He was still sniffling but someone had been kind enough to give him a lollipop and he was sucking on it sadly. Michael could see the grape stain on his lips. The guards brought Danny over to another cell, directly across from Michael.

"At least put him in with me, for God's sake," Michael said. "He's just a little kid."

Officer Joe shook his head. "Not a shot. He might be a little kid, but I've got explicit instructions to keep you two separated, though I think this whole thing is a load of crap. None of our guys have seen any sign of anything from this kid. All he did was bawl in the backseat." He stormed over to Michael's cell, his face so full of anger and disgust Michael stepped back fearfully. "But I will tell you this. I think it's despicable what your family has done. I love this country and would do anything for it, and to think your parents put me and my family in jeopardy." The officer glared at him.

Michael spoke softly. "I didn't kill anyone." He was stunned at this change of events. What people thought of him. What he was being accused of.

"Yeah, right. Lucky for you Hi-Core's coming. They've supposedly got lawyers coming out of their ears and are working with the FBI, Homeland Security, and anyone you can think of to find out the depths of depravity your family has committed. If Herrington wasn't so well lawyered, he'd be sitting where you are right now as well. Rotting in a jail cell, where you both belong in my opinion. Trust me, I won't lose any sleep thinking about you in a United States prison." He turned and opened the door to the containment area, pausing to put the keys back on the peg. One last look at them and he left, slamming the door shut behind him.

As soon as they were alone, Danny ran up to the bars of his cell and thrust his hands through. Realizing he couldn't reach his brother he sat on the cot and started to cry again.

Michael signed to him. "Are you okay, Birdman?"

Big tears ran down Danny's cheeks. "I want to be with you."

"I want to be with you, too, but the important thing to remember is we're both okay." He trudged around his cell. He had to come up with an idea, fast. He slammed his fist against the wall in frustration. What were they going to do? He'd promised Danny he wouldn't let anything happen to them, but here they were, locked up in jail cells and now everyone in the country thought he was a killer and Herrington's people were on the way to get him. Loneliness and despair washed over him, filling his heart with dread.

Frustrated, he paced his cell, when suddenly he had an idea. He snapped his fingers and turned to his brother. It was a long shot, but hell, why not give it a try?

"Danny, can you do anything else, besides talk to birds?"

Danny shrugged his shoulders.

Michael pressed him. "I mean, do you have any other powers I don't know about, yet? Can you move things with your mind or can you make people do things?"

Danny made a face and shook his head no.

He started pacing again. Think. Think. He sat on the bare cot and put his head in his hands. Sitting there, he felt a light breeze against his temple. He absently brushed aside a strand of hair on his forehead. Glancing up, he noticed the barred, narrow window against the far wall of his cell. He quickly ran over and peered out. There was only about five inches of space between the bars and Michael could only tilt his hand sideways and push it through. He groped around outside but all he could feel was the cold concrete and the cool outside air.

He turned back to Danny and started signing excitedly. "Danny, can you call birds to you if you needed to?"

Danny nodded. "But Mommy told me not to call them unless they come to me first. Unless she used the machine."

"The machine actually calls birds to you?" Michael asked.

Danny nodded. "Mommy says the waves call them, but I don't know what that means. But, I don't need the machine. I can still call them by myself. Mommy says the machine just finds the ones who are looking for the light the hardest. It sends out some really strong light stuff the birds look for, but I can make a light, too. Just like the machine. Do you want me to show you?"

"Yes. Do it, Danny. Call some really small birds to come help us. Remember—think small. They have to be able to fit through the window."

Danny walked over to his own window and put his hands together. He lowered his head and shut his eyes tight and Michael saw a bright yellow light emanate from his hands.

First it lit up his palms and then it spread quickly to his fingers until they were bathed in the light, the yellow splitting into the colors of the spectrum as they intertwined like rainbows between his fingers. Michael stood enthralled, amazed that his brother actually had the power to summon this type of magic. His gaze flitted to Danny's window and he gasped when a delicate little hummingbird, no more than four inches long from the tip of her bill to the tip of her tail, suddenly alighted on the windowsill in Danny's cell. Danny peered at his brother, smiling. "See, I told you I could do it. This is Mrs. Carmichael. Isn't she pretty?" He put his hand out. Mrs. Carmichael flew into the cell and perched gently on Danny's finger. "She saw the light and wants to know if I can send her there." He looked at Michael expectantly. "Can I?"

Michael shook his head. "Not yet. Can she understand me if I talk to her?"

The bird chirped and spread her wings.

"See, she understands you," signed Danny, one handed.

After getting over his initial shock, Michael spoke directly to the bird. "Mrs. Carmichael, we need your help. My brother can definitely send you on to the light, but first we need you to do us a favor. Some people have locked us up because they want to abuse the powers that Danny has. You know what he does is good. He can send people on to the light who can't find their way. We just need you to get us those keys hanging on the peg over there," he pointed. "If you can just bring them to me, I promise Danny will try to send you to the light."

The bird made no reaction. Michael turned to his brother. "Did she understand me?"

Danny shut his eyes and concentrated. Then he nodded. "She understands, but first she wants to know if the light is a good or bad place. She doesn't know, and that's why she hasn't tried to go there yet. She's scared."

Michael sighed and spoke to Mrs. Carmichael. "I wish I had an answer for you, but I don't. I really have no idea if the light is good or bad, but my brother has been able to see more of its qualities than anyone. He feels that it's a good place, a safe place everyone is drawn to. Is that what you're looking for?"

Mrs. Carmichael didn't move and Michael thought she didn't understand when suddenly she flew over to the peg and rested on its hook. There were five keys on the chain, which were well over half her size. The bird slowly shoved the key chain with her beak and feet and pushed it forward on the peg until it dropped to the floor. Then she flew down and dragged the chain, inch by inch, until Michael could reach his hands out through the cell bars and grab it from her.

"Thank you," he said, as he unlocked his cell door. Then, he ran over to Danny's and unlocked his as well. Both boys then turned to Mrs. Carmichael. "Are you ready to go?" Michael asked, gently.

Mrs. Carmichael sat in the hallway for some time, apparently making up her mind. Then, she slowly lifted and flew into Danny's outstretched hands where he gently cradled her shivering body. Danny closed his eyes and seemed to be whispering to the bird. Mrs. Carmichael relaxed in his palms.

Suddenly, a bright white light shot from his hands illuminating the room for a brief second and then quickly vanished.

Mrs. Carmichael's bird body immediately collapsed. Danny opened his eyes and glanced up at the window. Michael followed his gaze and could swear he saw a faint shadow shoot up out of his brother's hands and soar through the window.

Danny laid Mrs. Carmichael gently on the bunk and smiled. "She's happy. She told me so as she flew up to the light. She's not scared anymore."

Michael took a deep breath. "You did awesome, Birdman. Let's get out of here."

They made their way down the steps and started to tiptoe through the corridor on the right. That's when they heard the cops talking to someone on the phone.

"No, they're locked up good. There's no way they can get out." The officer paused, and then his voice rose up defensively. "No, I don't have anyone with them. I told you, I locked them up. What do you think they're gonna do? Fly away? They're steel bars." There was some more arguing and finally the officer slammed the phone down, exasperated. Michael heard him address another cop. "The folks at Hi-Core think the kids are gonna get out somehow. Do me a favor, Ray. Just take a look since the cameras are down. Gotta fix those things for times like this."

The other cop muttered something Michael couldn't hear, but he was sure it wasn't good.

Michael and Danny turned and instead of going back upstairs they ran down the hall going in the opposite direction. At the end of the corridor they came to a stairway and two long hallways jutted off, going left and right. Doors lined the two halls. Michael turned left, and tried each door, but all of them were locked.

He broke out in a desperate sweat, searching for someplace for them to hide when he heard Officer Ray running back down the stairs screaming at the top of his lungs. "Everyone, get out here now. They escaped."

Michael felt a tug on his elbow. Danny pointed to a door off to their left he hadn't noticed before. It was obstructed by a large metal garbage can. Michael ran over and moved the can aside and opened the door. It led into a storage room. He ushered Danny inside and locked the door, just as he heard the rest of the cops join in the hunt.

They moved farther into the room, searching for either a place to hide or a way out. He heard the officers run down the hall, trying the doors. "They didn't pass us so they must have come this way. Don't worry, they couldn't have gone far. Martinson, check the doors on the left. Walsh, check the ones on the right." Someone tried the storage room door.

"Hey, Joe!" someone yelled. "What's behind here?"

"It's the storage room. Why, is it locked?"

"Yeah, go get me the master keys. My key won't work on this lock. We've got to try every room in this hallway, locked or not. I'll bet my share of the five million they found a way into one of them. Hurry. Hi-Core's people will be here in less than an hour, and I want these kids found before they get here. I'm not going to have us blow five million dollars because of incompetence." Michael heard the man turn away from the door to try another one.

Frantically, he searched the room. The ceiling was lit by a row of emergency lights, enough to see his general surroundings. The room was overcrowded with equipment and storage shelves. He squeezed by a tall metal storage shelf which stretched across the entire room and stood nearly eight feet high. When he turned, he hit the edge of the next shelf with his shoulder. He couldn't imagine how the cops found anything in this place.

Looking up he saw the shelf next to him stacked high with ammonia bottles, buckets, sponges, and a whole assortment of products. Another ledge was lined with police uniforms. Everything from shirts and pants, to riot gear and all-purpose jackets.

The last unit was filled with survival gear. Flashlights, lanterns, dry food rations. Michael grabbed one of the flashlights and turned it on. The beam was strong. He searched through the piles for anything he could use to protect them. He found a pocketknife and grabbed it to replace the one the cop had taken from him, but he didn't feel it would be a good match against a gun. He also grabbed a can of Mace and stuffed it in his pocket.

Finally, he found something he thought might at least delay the officers for awhile—a blow up raft. Michael took it down and dragged it to the door. Then, after pushing Danny back so he wouldn't get in the way, he pulled on the cord. With a loud hiss, the raft inflated to a full five feet by nine feet. Michael wedged it in front of the door and ran back to the shelf for some industrial tape. He stretched it across the raft, securing it to the walls, the shelves, everything and anything that was near the door. Then he grabbed a metal file cabinet next to the wall and pushed it in front of the raft. Standing back, he paused, considering his work. If anyone tried to get in, they would first have to rip the raft away from the door and then get through all the other obstacles. He turned, staring around the room and trying to figure out how he was going to get out of it.

In the distance, Michael heard the cops coming back, the hollow echo of their shoes on the tile floor growing louder as they neared. The sound of keys jingling made his skin crawl.

He swept the flashlight around the room again and in the far upper left hand corner of the ceiling he saw a hole in the tiles. He jumped over some boxes to get a better look. The flashlight showed him that the entire ceiling was suffering water damage and many of the tiles were lying on the floor. Above, just like in the movies, there seemed to be an air conditioning vent lined with piping which ran above the ceiling. They didn't have much choice.

"Danny, come here."

Danny ran over while Michael climbed up one of the metal-shelving units. Halfway up, he turned and signed again to Danny. "Grab my hand and crawl up me. I'll lift you into the hole and then I'll follow you, okay?"

Danny nodded.

There was a muffled grunt as one of the cops tried to open the storage room door. Michael's barricade was working. The door wouldn't give.

"Dammit, what the hell is wrong with this lock?" Michael heard the cop ask. "Did you give me the right keys?"

Without waiting to hear more, Michael took a deep breath and, yanking on Danny's arm, helped him to climb up and then pushed him into the narrow space. The shelving unit tottered under his weight and he practically threw his brother into the vent and through the ceiling tiles, which crumbled like paper-mache and scattered all around him. Once Danny was safely through, Michael hoisted himself onto the shelf as far as he could and grabbed onto the pipes, pulling himself through the narrow opening. It was tight for Danny, but worse for him. His jeans ripped against the notches on the pipe and his shoulders were crushed against the sides of the vent. This was not like the movies where you simply crawled through a clean, smooth aluminum tube.

Michael patted Danny on his rump and his brother moved tentatively further, balancing himself on top of the pipes.

There was a sudden sharp cracking sound, like an axe being hit against the door, and he knew he had to hurry. He shined his flashlight in the direction he wanted Danny to go. They crawled another fifteen feet before Michael heard the officers finally get into the storage room and a loud explosion as the raft blew apart. The officer's shouts to search the room echoed through the vent, bouncing off the aluminum walls.

Michael glanced down at a light coming from the grating vent below him and saw a row of urinals and green and white floor tile. He tugged on Danny's foot to get his attention and then lifted the grate, lowering himself into the bathroom, squeezing through the opening like toothpaste trying to get through the tube. He hung from the pipe and jumped the extra four feet to the ground.

"Come on, Danny, I'll catch you," he signed, as Danny balanced from above. First, Danny let his legs dangle, and then he dropped sideways into Michael's arms, pushing him close to the floor from the force.

"Let's get out of here," Michael said, standing up. He partially opened the door to get a view of the outside hall. They were back in the original passageway, right next to the stairs, which led up to the cells. No one was in sight, but Michael could hear the cops around the corner, cursing in the storage room. Michael grabbed Danny's hand and they quietly made their way out into the hall and past the room where they had first heard the cop speaking to Herrington's men on the phone.

The hallway twisted again, but Michael could now see exit signs in bold, neon red and followed them outside.

Once free, Michael headed quickly for the two police cruisers in the lot. He felt conspicuous in the well-lit area and moved fast. Unfortunately, both of the cars were locked. "Damn, I was hoping we could use these."

As Michael thought of what to do, he heard motors approaching. He grabbed Danny and they raced around the side of the building, where they wouldn't be seen from the road.

Within seconds, two brown sedans came barreling around the bend and pulled up in front of the entrance. Danny grabbed Michael's arm as he watched two uniformed officers from one car and one from the other storm out and, with guns drawn, run up the steps, entering the jail. Michael fumed. There were no Hi-Core agents. These people were Herrington's people, even though decals on the side of the sedans said Hi-Core Industries. He recognized the two officers named Garrett and Carol immediately.

Michael could see into the driver's side of each vehicle. The agents had left one driver in the first sedan.

"Now's our only chance, Danny," Michael explained. "We have to get out of here and we need a getaway car. We'll never be able to outrun them on foot."

He grabbed the bottle of mace from his pocket and placed his finger lightly on the trigger. "Follow me."

They crept around the outside perimeter of the sedan and came up from the back. The driver's gaze was trained on the front entrance and he never saw them approach.

Michael's adrenaline raced as he squeezed close by the window, pressing firmly against the side door. He tapped on the glass.

Surprised to see someone in his rear view mirror, the driver opened his door and Michael sprayed the man's face. The driver screamed and fell out of the car, holding his hands up to shield his eyes. Michael dropped the Mace and landed two hard kicks—one in the guy's stomach and the next against the side of his head. While the driver lay on the ground screaming and covering his face, Michael grabbed Danny and pushed him into the front seat. He jumped in, slammed the door shut, and put the car in reverse. At the same moment, Michael could see activity inside the building through the large glass windows next to the front door. All the cops were running outside. As soon as Herrington's people saw their driver lying on the ground, they started firing at the car, trying to blow out the tires to stop him from escaping, but they were too far away. Michael briefly noticed the startled expressions of the real cops as they watched Herrington's people shooting at kids.

Without waiting to see more, Michael pushed Danny down into the floor well, then threw the car into drive and sped down the road. They were going to get less than a minute's head start. He was determined to make it a good one. After a half a mile, the road emptied onto a two-lane country highway.

Michael quickly brought the car up to ninety miles an hour and tore down the road, completely blind as to where they were headed. After what seemed like mere seconds, he could see through his rearview mirror the other sedan and two police cruisers barrel out of the side road onto the highway, their sirens and lights on full blast. They were going fast.

"Will they catch us?" Danny signed, from the floor well in the front seat.

Michael shook his head furiously, not daring to take his hands from the wheel to answer. He leaned over and shut off his headlights so they wouldn't be seen, driving in the dark with only the faint moonlight as his guide. The road curved to the right and they were out of view of the pursuing vehicles for the moment. Then a gift. The moon came out of the clouds for a brief instant and he saw it. About fifty feet ahead, on the left, a side road came into view. He immediately hit the brakes so he could make the turn. Unfortunately, they still didn't slow down enough and Michael had to attempt a wide arc to make the side road, causing a sickening two-wheel careen. The car screeched and teetered on the brink of overturning and then crashed back on all four wheels.

Swallowing back bile, Michael floored the gas pedal and pushed the car hard down the side road. He risked turning on the lights for a second, saw what he needed, and turned sharply to the right and then up a wooded hill. After a few more seconds, the road made another sharp right and Michael could now see directly onto the two-lane highway. He immediately cut the lights and engine and within thirty seconds he saw the other vehicles come into view. None of them made the turn-off. Instead, they headed straight along the highway, full speed. They hadn't been seen.

Michael watched, dumbfounded, as the taillights receded from view. He sat back against the seat and took a shuddering breath. He glanced at Danny cowering in the well. "Come on, Birdman. Let's get you in the front seat."

He helped Danny up and fastened his seatbelt.

Michael restarted the engine and turned the car around, back down the hill to the highway, retracing the way they had come. They drove past the turnoff where the cops had taken them and down the highway, straight into nowhere. Michael waited a full five minutes before he even put the headlights back on.

They rode for almost an hour before they saw another car. For a while he felt like he and Danny were the only people left on the planet. Open highway, no lights, and solitude. Finally, Michael saw a sign for a town called Kimball. Within fifteen minutes they were there, and Michael pulled into the first parking lot he saw. It was for the local grocery store and there was a large sign out front with a cow on it saying, "Come in, our prices are moo-ving! Milk for only $1.99 a carton!"

Thankfully it was closed. Michael parked the sedan at the far end of the lot, shaded by a group of trees, and unfastened Danny from the harness in the front seat, where he had fallen asleep and leaned him against the door, using his jacket as a pillow. After he was sure the doors were locked, Michael leaned back on the front seat and closed his eyes, half expecting to hear the other cars come up behind them, but none came. He felt so drained and spent after what had just happened he couldn't even think anymore. After about five minutes, his body finally won out over his fear and he fell asleep.

Chapter Thirteen

Day 7 Sunday, 7:30 a.m.

Michael was shaken roughly awake and cried out when he saw his mother flashed before his eyes. It took him a moment before he realized Danny was holding a photo of her and had shoved it in his face. As he tried to calm his breathing, his brother crawled into his lap and began taking out picture after picture from a large burlap bag he had found in the backseat. His stomach churned. There were hundreds of photos of his family. Recent ones and others as much as twenty years old.

He thrust his hand into the bag and scooped up some of the pictures at the bottom of the pile, seeing images and scenes he hadn't thought about in years. Suddenly, he was blinded by rage, knowing he'd been spied on his entire life. The analogy of feeling like a goldfish in a glass bowl fit him to a tee.

One picture stood out from the others. It was 5 x 7, frayed around the edges. A young couple held a baby in front of a birthday cake lit with one candle. It was his mother and father, but they were so very young and looked so different. They were outside on a backyard patio, the ocean in the background. His mother was wearing a halter-top and flowery skirt and his dad was in Bermuda shorts. Banana and coconut trees framed the background of the shot. Michael stared at the smiling baby in his mother's arms, seeing his own green eyes staring back at him.

They seemed so happy, his father beaming at the camera and his mother grinning at him. It made his heart ache. What shook him, though, were the guests around the table next to them. Dobber was there, holding out a wrapped gift and there in the corner of the photo was none other than Herrington himself, sitting on a lawn chair, his fingers tented as if he were in deep concentration.

So it was true. His parents really were spies and Herrington really was a bad guy, not just an eccentric scientist. Through all of this Michael simply hadn't wanted to believe it, hadn't really allowed his mind to accept that his parents were anything but what they claimed to be. But this picture proved it. He sat back, feeling numb and cold and more in shock than at any other time throughout this entire ordeal.

Still, it didn't change who he was. It didn't mean he was a spy. It didn't mean he was innately bad. My god, he had found a wallet the year before during Christmastime filled with over five hundred dollars inside and found the owner, returning it immediately!

He watched his brother sift through picture after picture, completely unaware of what he was really seeing. Photos of his mother and father in labs, sitting at dinner with

Herrington, laughing at the camera. He knew his brother was just happy to see pictures of himself—any normal six-year-old would be, but Michael was certain he didn't know what it really meant.

Disgusted, he turned to the backseat and was surprised to see on the floor various pieces of computer equipment and a cell phone. Staring at it gave him an idea and he reached over and picked up the phone. It was Sunday, but just maybe he'd be there. The guy was a workaholic.

Amazingly it wasn't locked. Michael dialed 0 and was connected to an operator. "I was wondering if you could help me," he asked. "I need to get in touch with a teacher from Rockland County High School in Spring Valley, New York, and I don't have the phone number. Would you be able to get it for me? I really need to reach this man. It's very important."

"I'm sorry, sir," the operator said. "We don't offer phone listings at this service. Let me connect you to the local information center in that area. For future reference the area code is 845. Please hold on."

Michael waited for about thirty seconds when suddenly a new voice came on. "Hello, what is your listing, please?"

"I need the phone number for Rockland County High School in Spring Valley, New York," he said, looking around for a pen and anything to write on. On the backseat he saw a notebook with a pencil attached to it by a rubber band. He grabbed it, scribbled down the number on the first page of the book and thanked the operator. After hanging up the phone, he glanced back down at the page, confused. He started rifling through the notebook.

Page after page was filled with numbers. After each number was a series of notes. He quickly scanned through the rest of the pages and at the back of the book he saw something he didn't expect to see.

He stamped his foot on the floor, getting his brother's attention. "Hey, Danny, what's Mom doing with you? What's this in the picture?" He showed him the book with a photo of his mother and Danny sitting on the floor of their living room with a large black rectangular box in front of them. It looked recent.

"It's just the machine," he signed, as he looked at the photograph. "She's trying to adjust it so it's stronger."

Michael stared at the picture. The box had dials stationed across it and about fifteen small light bulbs. Nearly half of them were lit. Danny sat on the floor next to the box with a large headset over his ears.

"What are you wearing?"

"Super hearing robot parts," he explained, smiling. "When Mommy puts the robot parts on me she turns on the machine, and we try to see how far I can see."

"What do you mean, how far you can see?"

"Each level I move up to means I'm getting stronger," he explained. "When I was little I could only get to level three. Now Mommy says I'm up to level thirteen. Two more and she says I'll be just like Superman."

"Yeah, like Superman," Michael said, angrily. Whether it was for his well-being or not, he was hurt his parents didn't respect him enough to let him in on what was going on. If they had, maybe none of this would have happened and maybe he could have done something to prevent putting Danny in danger. Michael looked at the machine. How had they kept it a secret for so long? To think this machine was actually in his house someplace and he had never laid eyes on it his entire life.

He sat back on the front seat and took a deep breath, trying to relax, but it was hard. He kept clenching and unclenching his fists. Still, being angry wasn't going to get him anywhere. He had to get back some control of the situation, and information was the only way to do that. He needed to learn everything he possibly could about Danny's powers and maybe he could find some way to use it to their advantage. It had already worked at the police station, so maybe there was more he could do.

"Hey, Danny, explain this to me," he started. It was obvious Danny's powers were connected to this black box, but the question was, how? Was the machine responsible for his brother's powers or did it just aid him along? Obviously, he didn't need the machine to do everything. So what else was there? What was Herrington really after? It couldn't be just a black box with light bulbs on it, could it? For God's sake, he could build another machine.

He continued his questions. "So Mom was helping you get stronger so you could reach level fifteen? And she used the box to help you get there?"

Danny nodded.

"Did she say what would happen when you finally got to level fifteen?"

"She said I'd be able to see right into where the people go."

Michael stared at him skeptically. "See where they go? Do you mean...see into Heaven? The light?"

Danny nodded.

Like turning on the lights after sitting in the dark for hours, his realization was both exhilarating and painful. Michael suddenly understood everything. It wasn't the box Herrington was after—it was the true meaning of life and death. Danny was the only person who he seemed to believe could offer proof of an afterlife, the very light that everyone spoke about. It wasn't just about controlling souls, but controlling Heaven. He stared at his brother, so innocent in his ignorance about possessing the most incredible power known to man. How much more did he know?

"Danny, if you get a chance to see Heaven, what could you do there?"

Danny shrugged his shoulders. "I don't know. Mommy said I'd learn more about my powers once I got there and I'm getting really close. She said she thought the birds would tell me what to do once I'm there. Can I go back and look at the pictures some more?"

What a time for him to lose interest in the conversation. "Sure, Birdman, go on and look at the pictures."

Within seconds Danny was once more engrossed in the photographs of his family.

Michael turned towards the phone again and dialed the number of the high school, at first, pleasantly surprised when they answered. "Administration office, how can I help you?" an elderly voice said.

Then, he groaned, recognizing the voice as Miss Scribbner's—the office secretary who had been working at the high school for over thirty-five years. She was a cranky, bitter old maid and was not known to be a lover of students. Why they kept her on staff at all was a complete mystery and the students hated her.

"Hello, Miss Scribbner," he said, trying to be as polite as possible. "This is Michael Anderson. I'm a student in my senior year at Rockland."

Her reaction was not what he expected. "Oh, my, Michael Anderson. Yes, I know you." Her voice got very stern. "The things they are accusing you of. You are going to have to answer for a lot of things, young man."

Michael could hear her shrill voice getting higher and higher as she spoke. "I didn't do any of that stuff, Miss Scribbner. Please, do you know if Mr. Daley, the biology teacher, is in? It's important I talk to him."

He could hear Miss Scribbner mumbling to herself on the other end of the line, debating about what to do. He interrupted her thoughts, pleading with her. "Miss Scribbner, it's really important I speak with him."

"You're lucky the school is even open today because of the Key Club event and all the end of year testing, which I might add you are missing, young man. And now the FBI is scouring the school in the off chance you'll show up. In fact, I'm going to tell them right now you're on the phone."

"Fine, go ahead and call them, but connect me to Mr. Daley first. Please, I'm begging you."

There was a long pause while Miss Scribbner must have been deciding what to do Michael thought. He was about to give up when he heard the intercom in the background requesting that Mr. Daley please come down to the administration office immediately.

He breathed a sigh of relief.

"Michael, you may be on hold for a while so don't hang up," she instructed. "In the meantime, I'm going to contact the authorities."

"Fine." He waited anxiously. It felt like he had been waiting forever, even though it was actually only two minutes. Then, a familiar voice came on the line.

"Hello?"

Michael could barely speak, his voice choking up on him with relief. It was Daley.

"Hello? Miss Scribbner said a student was on the phone for me. Either speak or I'm going to hang up."

Michael couldn't get the words out fast enough. "No, don't hang up. It's me, Mr. Daley. Michael Anderson."

He heard Daley draw in a startled breath. "Michael, is that really you? Oh, my God, son, how are you?"

"I'm okay," he said and then, without warning he stifled back a sob. It was more from relief than fear, just knowing he was finally able to talk to someone he trusted. Daley must not have read it that way and Michael immediately heard the worry in his voice.

"Michael, are you sure you're okay? Is Danny all right?"

"Danny's fine," he said. "Mr. Daley, they think I killed Mr. Jacobs, my Scout Master and some kid at a convenience store. I swear I didn't do any of that."

"I know, Michael. I know. Tell me, where are you right now? Have you been able to make contact yet with the person I sent you to?"

"No, I haven't made it there yet. This thing we're involved in is so much bigger than you know." Michael's voice rose, got faster. "My parents are spies working for Samuel Herrington, and they've been doing experiments on my brother. Now, these other agents are posing as policemen, and the whole country is after us. Even the cops are in on it. I'm serious. They captured Danny and me at a roadblock someplace outside of California and took us to a jail cell so they could trade us to Hi-Core Industries who had put a bounty on our heads! I can't even trust the police. I don't know what to do."

"It's okay, Michael. It's okay," Daley soothed. "You're doing a wonderful job. Tell me, have you by any chance heard any word from your parents?"

Michael was startled. "No, how could I?" He thought of the condor, but suddenly doubted if it had even been his father. And what—he was going to come out and tell Daley that yes, his dad was about to be killed and might be a bird? He was suddenly angry again. "And even if I did hear from them, why should I believe anything they say? My parents are liars."

Daley chuckled softly. "Actually, you're right about that."

Michael was shocked. "You know what I'm talking about?"

"It would be hard not to. You're still front-page news here, kid. Suspected spies children on the run for their lives, go the headlines. Actually, you might be interested to hear the FBI just released new information about this case. It's now a felony for any American, policeman, or civilian, to profit by turning you and your brother over to Hi-Core Industries instead of someone from the government. Because of the kidnapping of your parents, the attack at the Plaza, the bombing of your house, and the subsequent killings of American citizens, this is now an internal matter and Homeland Security has gotten involved to investigate." He paused. "The most important thing though, Michael, is that, incredibly, your parents have been cleared. The United States government no longer thinks they're spies for Herrington. Let's give this one to the president for doing the right thing."

Michael sat up straight in the seat. "How can that be? All the evidence clearly indicates they had dealings with him the entire time. What about them supposedly disappearing for five years, the money they came back with? Selling drugs and hiding information?"

"Michael, as far as the public is now concerned, they're being told your parents were working on some secret government contra-terrorism experiments. Things which would help us in case of a global bio-agent attack. That we made them disappear, and they were paid well for their participation. People will believe what they read and hear and if the journalists do their job right, your parents are going to come out as heroes. And I'm sure soon you'll be cleared as well from all the charges against you."

"Heroes? Are you sure?"

"It's true, Michael. The government actually found all the documents supposedly sent to Herrington, and it was all false information."

"I heard about those documents before," Michael said. "This guy who works with my parents, named Dobber, called me at home, the morning after the attack at the Plaza, and then again when we were at a motel. I've known this man my entire life and he told me he could help me, but he lied. He was the one who turned us in, set Herrington's agents on us and I barely escaped. I can't trust anyone, Mr. Daley. I bet this line is even tapped. I have to look out for my brother and everyone we've put our trust into has turned on us or been killed."

"I know it's been hard for you, but there's going to be a time, very soon, when you'll have to put your trust in someone, and I'm glad you put it in me to get you out of Rockland," he said. "You can't do this all alone. You don't have the resources to stay out of sight indefinitely. You need to get into the right hands, fast."

"Well, how am I going to do that?" Michael asked. "Every time we try, everything falls apart. Please, Mr. Daley, is there anything you can do for us? Can you call someone for me? Get your friend to come to me? Get police who don't want to lock me up? I just don't know who to turn to anymore."

Mr. Daley paused for a moment, then spoke quickly. "Michael, I want you to listen to me very carefully, because what I'm going to say next will change the way you look at everything. That guy, Dobber? He didn't turn you in. The agents in the sedans found you on their own using the tracking device that was in Danny's ear. Dobber really was trying to help you. He actually works for the FBI."

Michael was stunned and couldn't find his voice. "How could you possibly know that?" he asked, hushed. "And, how do you know about the tracking device?" Fear flooded Michael. No, not Daley, too.

"I just know." Daley's voice took on a different tone. "Michael, hang on a sec."

Michael heard a muffled conversation and Daley came back on. "Listen, I need you to call me at a different number in half an hour at a different location. Will you do that? Just reverse the charges and I'll accept."

What he said next chilled Michael to the bone. "More importantly, I want you and Danny out of that car as soon as possible. If we could track you there from this phone call, then I'm sure Herrington's people will be on to you soon."

Michael felt like the world had just been pulled out from under his feet. He looked over at Danny, scared to death. "How did you know where I was?" he whispered. "I never told you. Are you one of them too, Mr. Daley?" No, this couldn't be happening.

"Kid, I said you were going to have to trust someone and that someone is me. What's going on is that I work for the FBI, have for the past twenty years," he declared. "I'll explain everything to you later. Now, once I give you the number I want you to get out of that car and get someplace where you can get a phone call out to me. Here's the number, do you have a pen and paper?"

"I think so," Michael said shakily. He felt numb. Daley worked for the FBI? This was more than he could take. It all had to be a mistake. He heard Daley talking to him, but it was as if it was from far away. Suddenly, he didn't want to listen to him anymore, didn't want to listen to anyone. Everything he knew to be true was being twisted in a horrible, cruel way. He closed his eyes and heard a strange buzzing in his ears, as if a bee was continuously flying around his head in circles. He almost laughed, thinking this was what it must feel like to have a stroke.

He heard Daley yelling at him through the phone lines, forcing him back to reality. "Michael, are you listening to me? Come on, kid, answer me already."

He shook his head, trying to clear it. God, he was so tired. "I'm here, I'm here, I hear you," he mumbled.

"Thank, God. Look, I know this is a lot for you to handle, but you don't have a choice right now. There's too much depending on your getting through this, so don't flake out on me. Now, get your pen and paper and write this down. I'm pretty sure this line is secure, but there are too many other prying ears around here and I don't want them to know this number. Now, the first three digits in the phone number are the numbers for the second animal we dissected this year in class. Got that?"

No, he didn't. Again, he felt like he was on stage where everyone knew the joke except him. "Mr. Daley, what are you talking about? I don't understand what this has to do with my biology class. I don't understand what this has to do with anything."

"It's a code, kid. You're smart, figure it out," he said. "Now, the next three numbers are all for the amount of fish in the aquarium. The next number is for the total amount of girls in your biology class and the last three numbers are for the amount of money I gave you in the envelope. Now, ditch the car and go. When you leave the parking lot, walk north. There's a bowling alley about a quarter mile away. Go inside and call me from a pay phone there. Half an hour, got that?"

"No, I don't got that," he yelled, but the line had gone dead.

Michael stared at the phone in his hand. Slowly, the implications of what he had just learned hit him hard. Daley had known they were in the car because he had traced him through the cellphone lines. If what Miss Scribbner said was true, then the FBI really was all over the school and had put taps on the phone lines. Michael was stunned to think they knew him well enough to know he would eventually call the school. A school where Mr. Daley apparently was more than a plain old biology teacher. If that was true, then it meant Mr. Daley had been in on everything from the moment he first met him. Maybe even sending him on a phony goose chase to California, anything to get him on the run. The thought made his skin crawl. It also meant if the FBI could track them, then he was sure Herrington's people could, too. This was their car, after all. He sprang into action.

"Danny, we've got to leave, right now."

"Can I take some of the pictures with me?"

"Sure, grab a few and let's go."

Danny shuffled through them, considering, and then picked up three photos, folded them up and put them in his jacket pocket.

As Michael opened the back door of the car and helped Danny out, the cell phone rang. Curiously, he went over to it. Instinct told him not to pick it up, but the urge of the ringing phone was too strong. It might be Daley, calling him back to tell him something else. He picked up the receiver.

It wasn't Daley.

"Hello, Michael." He didn't recognize the cold, dead voice on the line. "You're more resilient than I thought. You keep eluding my men, though after doing a psychological profile run on you, it appears people around you have never given you the respect you deserve, have they? I could use someone like you on my team."

"Mr. Herrington?" Michael asked, his voice hushed.

"Yes, it's me. Now listen, I want to make you a deal. I have your parents, they're alive and well, but I need information from you only your brother can supply. Bring him to me and I promise I'll release all of you. Get you set up somewhere safe, new names, new identities and we can all start over. I did this once for your parents, and I promise to do it again."

Suddenly, Michael heard someone scream out in the background and his heart leapt into his chest. It was his mother. "Don't listen to him, Michael. He's a liar. Run away with Danny. Protect yourselves." He heard a loud commotion, chairs being overturned, and then silence.

Michael started screaming hysterically. "Don't you hurt my mother. Leave her alone."

Herrington shrieked, "Danny is my property. I have invested millions into this research, and I am going to get results with or without your parents. Bring him to me or I'll kill your parents!"

"I will never give you my brother."

"Then your parents will die."

Michael screamed in frustration and slammed down the cellphone, his anger and rage maxed to the ultimate limit. Crazed, he picked up a laptop from the floor well and threw it against the car door, shattering the window. He couldn't get his mother's cries out of his head, knowing she was trapped and there was nothing he could do for her. Suddenly, he heard a piece of metal fall to the floor outside the car. Michael grabbed the paper with the phone number code words and jumped out. There on the ground was the smallest satellite dish he'd ever seen. It fit into the palm of his hand and had been attached to the side of the car. Now he knew how everyone had tracked him. He started stomping on it with his foot until it was nothing but a small broken heap of metal pieces. He turned to Danny who was cringing.

"Danny, c'mon," he signed, the anger from his tantrum not abating for an instant.

They took off across the parking lot, while Michael got his bearings. The sun was to his right and rising. Right in front of him was a road. It was heading north. "This way."

They reached the bowling alley in five minutes. Michael ushered Danny inside, got change for a dollar and sent Danny to the game room to play pinball. Going to a pay phone nearby, where he still had a good view of his brother, he took out the code sheet. He had calmed down enough to think rationally again, but it was hard. His mother's screaming voice kept echoing through his head. He was thankful she was still alive, but he knew she was in deep trouble. Michael tried not to imagine the face of the horrible man who held her hostage and instead, started imagining the multiple ways he'd make them pay for hurting his parents.

He shook his head and took out the paper with Daley's directions, staring dumbly at the first question. It made no sense to him. "The second animal we dissected in class was a pig," Michael mused. Could he have meant that there are three letters in the word pig? He wrote down the numbers 3-3-3. He thought about it for a while and realized he'd never heard of an area code starting with three of the same digit. Suddenly he understood. He took a closer look at the phone and matched up the numbers to the letters on the dial spelling the word pig. The first three numbers were 7, which corresponded to the letter P, 4 for I and 4 for G.

The next three numbers represented the amount of fish in the aquarium. As of two weeks ago there had been three but one of them had died after getting sucked into the filter after someone didn't set it back up properly after cleaning it. That left two. Michael glanced again at the phone. He spelled out the word two and matched the numbers. 8-9-6. The next number was for the number of girls in his class, which were nine and Mr. Daley had given Michael exactly four hundred dollars in the envelope. Did that mean he should spell out the number nine? That would have been four letters right there, but it didn't make sense because he wouldn't have to use the last question Daley posed. Sitting back he thought about it some more and tried the number nine and then added 400 from the next question. That meant the number was 744-896-9400.

Satisfied, he went over to the game room and watched Danny playing an old Addams Family pinball machine. Though he couldn't hear anything, he seemed to sense what to do and laughed happily when Thing came out and gave him an extra ball. Michael waited until Danny's game was over and then took him to the commissary where he bought them each a hot dog, some fries, and a coke.

Danny suddenly stopped eating and stared at his brother. "Will we ever see Mommy and Daddy again?"

It was a question he had asked himself many times over the past few days. "I hope so, Danny. I really do."

"But why can't I go see them? Is it because of me? Did I do something wrong?"

"No, you didn't do anything wrong. None of this is your fault." He tilted his brother's chin up to face him. "Danny, what you can do with the birds is a wonderful and incredible thing. You have a special power, and there are bad people who want to know how you do it."

"But I can tell them how to do it," he answered. "Maybe they'll let Mommy and Daddy come home then."

"I don't think it'll be that easy," he signed, wincing as he thought again of his mother screaming on the other end of the line, wondering what Herrington was going to do to her. "Listen, I need to make a phone call to Mr. Daley, the nice teacher who helped us out and gave us his car." Teacher, yeah right. "You want to come with me?"

Danny nodded, and they both went over to the phone booth. Michael took out the number from his pocket, dialed and had the operator reverse the charges. Immediately, Daley picked up.

"Hey, kid, how ya doing?"

Michael involuntarily started laughing. "Oh, just fine, great, super, in fact. Um, I'm sorry about your car. The police that nabbed us took it."

"Don't worry about it," he chuckled. "It wasn't mine anyway. Listen, now that we're on an untapped line we can talk more freely. Too many ears over at the high school. I know this is a shock for you to hear I'm actually from the FBI, but you've had so many shocks the past few days, I can't imagine this one will throw you any worse than the others.

"What I need is for you to get me up to speed on what you know. When you came to me back at the school I had no choice but to give you my car and send you as far away as possible. I didn't have the resources at the time to help you. Especially with that mob on your tail.

"We thought we'd be able to track you through the device implanted in Danny's ear, but it seems you got rid of that a few days ago. Not bad, kid, not bad."

Michael interrupted him. "Mr. Daley, before we talk about anything, you have to clear up something for me. I don't understand what's going on. I mean, you're my biology teacher. How can you be involved in the government? How can you even know about the microchip in Danny's ear? It doesn't make sense."

"It actually makes a lot of sense. I work for the government and years ago I was assigned to monitor you."

Michael was stunned. "Monitor me? Why?"

"For safety reasons, mostly. Sit back, because what I'm going to tell you next is going to be a big surprise. Your family doesn't work for Herrington. They work for us, the FBI. When they were growing up, both of your parents proved to be brilliant mathematicians, scoring the highest grades in their schools each and every time they took a standardized test. They were just teenagers and were sought out by the government to assist them with a top-secret investigation. They were perfect moles. Both of their parents had died very young, and they each had no brothers or sisters. Your mother was actually living with a foster family in Queens when the government first came to her with their proposal."

Michael was shocked. "My mother was an orphan?" He had never heard this before. "Are you sure?"

"Absolutely. I've reviewed your parent's files and have known both of them for many, many years. When your father was growing up, he lived in Florida with an old friend of his mother's. Unfortunately, she passed away almost eight years ago."

"Unbelievable," Michael whispered.

Mr. Daley continued. "When your mother was thirteen and your father was fourteen, the government approached your parents and proposed a wonderful opportunity. The chance to work for the United States Government and serve their country. All their schooling would be paid for and they would be economically sound for the rest of their lives.

"It was an offer they couldn't refuse. It was the chance of a lifetime, a chance for them both to truly belong to a family of people who all believed in the same thing. The safety and security of the United States.

"Your parents were sent to live in D.C. where they started school studying bio-physics, pathological warfare, toxicology, you name it. They became excellent neurophysicists and all of this was to get them to infiltrate Samuel Herrington's organization where we could find out what this man was really doing. He's one of the most lethal men in the world and while the government does a good spin on him, trying to play down his deadliness to the public, this man can destroy the human race a thousand times over with any of the strains of viruses he has at his disposal. His influence has become global and he has heads of states in various countries answering to him.

"The year your parents received their doctorates, we set them up in a top lab at a university, putting their work in the news. It was only a matter of time before Herrington's people came looking for them. He's always on the prowl for brilliance and to find ways to harvest it. He flew your parents to Europe to talk with him, showed him his labs, basically gave them everything a scientist would ever want, which is the ability to have the funds and means to do their research at their pace and their own way. As long as they also worked on his side agenda, which was to find out what happened to people when they die. It's one of the overriding missions of his organization. And now that his wife's dying, he's desperate to know what's going to happen to her.

"So, with our blessing, they accepted Herrington's offer and moved to an island facility far in the Pacific for five years, fell in love, got married, and had you. When they were trained in everything Herrington wanted, he moved them back to a lab in New York and they continued their research. All the time he thought they were working for him, but they were really counter agents working for the FBI and we had to keep that secret at all costs. For the next few years, everything proceeded according to plan."

"And the plan was what?" Michael asked.

"The plan was to gain access to Herrington's secret terrorist activity and scientific technology and to integrate themselves deeply into the entire political, ethical and biochemical culture through their scientific connections. Their main focus was contra terrorism, supplying us information to fight against anything Herrington had created. In fact, because of your parents, we have in our labs right now antidotes to dozens of viruses Herrington's people have manufactured and because of your parents, if Herrington decided to release any of these strains into the environment, the United States people and others around the globe could be treated. Michael, your parents really are brilliant, amazing people—true heroes."

"So what happened?" Michael asked.

"Nothing for years, but then Herrington's wife became ill and he was desperate about her impending death, so he started to focus on your parents. He wanted to know what was going to happen to Marta. Really happen. Not just the idea of a heaven or hell, but the true meaning of what will happen to her soul when she dies. Where will she go? What will happen to her? Your parents were the only ones working on the life after death scenarios, so he concentrated on them and even though they hadn't come up with any conclusions, he was desperate. But that was when his people realized something odd was happening and maybe things weren't as they appeared. There were too many birds surrounding your house, seemingly centered around your brother. So, as with anything unusual, even if it might mean nothing, Herrington's people were told to constantly be on watch and subsequently started surveillance on your family. Once that happened, they saw your mother working with Danny and the machine. Nothing in their research or findings reported on this device and Herrington then knew your parents were hiding things from him."

"But my parents did send information back to Herrington at times. Wasn't that treasonous?"

"Everything they turned over to Herrington was carefully screened by the FBI first. We had to make it look as if your parents were really working for him, but we never sent anything which wouldn't have been released to the public sooner or later. Herrington thought he was getting in on the inside, but nothing he received had any bearing on what he really needed or wanted. And, all those business trips they had over the years? They were meeting with Herrington and other labs around the globe. But the end agenda was to find the ultimate answer."

"About what happens to you when you die."

"That's right. There's always been talk of a light people see when they die. Herrington's main agenda for your parents was to use all their resources to see if there really was a connection between death and the bright light everyone says they see and could the experience be simulated in a laboratory. When your mother was pregnant with Danny, she was accidentally hit with a dangerous amount of ultraviolet rays. Luckily, she came away basically unharmed, but your parents were more concerned about your brother. When he was born, he seemed healthy, but by the time he was only a few months old, they knew something was very different about him. He didn't look at them when they spoke to him, slept through thunderstorms, hardly ever cried. But, even more, it was the way he'd stare out the window, watching the sky all the time, as if he were searching for something. Then your parents learned of your brother's abilities and they got scared. They had Dobber place an implant in his ear so if Herrington ever decided to take Danny, they could track him."

"So Dobber worked for you the whole time, too?" Michael asked.

"Yes, your parents suggested to Herrington that he would be a valuable asset to his organization and Dobber defected, so to speak."

"I don't understand something," Michael said. "If Herrington is this uber bad guy, why haven't you arrested him yet? Why do you let him continue to do his illegal dealings around the world?"

Daley sighed. "It's complicated. There are times you want the bad guys to be visible bad guys. We know some of the atrocities Herrington is doing, but at the same time, by having your parents in his organization, we can learn about all the horrors he's done in the past. Just getting rid of him isn't the answer yet. He has lethal drugs hidden in labs all over the globe and accomplices who are very loyal to him. The fear is if we just remove him, there may be orders and fail safes in place to do away with the rest of the world. We need to be sure that won't happen."

"Why did Dobber lie to me?"

"Dobber couldn't tell you the entire truth at the time because it would have only confused you. There was just too much for you to have to accept so soon," Daley explained. "He tried to tell you what he thought you would need to know. Just enough for you to believe him and listen to him."

Michael sat back on the seat. "I thought Dobber was a traitor and turned us in to those fake cops. Back at one of the motels he told me to wait and he would come for us, and I believed him. No more than one minute later Herrington's people pulled up. We barely got out in time."

"I know, Michael. It seems they found out about the tracking device and honed in on the frequency. Dobber didn't know how much time he had and wanted to get to you as soon as possible. It's a good thing you ran and an even better one you removed the device. I tracked you both until you were picked up outside California."

"What?" Anger rolled through Michael. "If you knew where we were the whole time, why didn't you come for us? What were you waiting for? They could have taken my brother at any time."

"Michael, we did try to come for you. We'd been tracking you in the car, but we also tracked you with the credit card back in Pennsylvania," he explained. "If we could locate you, then we were sure Herrington's people were on to your whereabouts as well. We didn't want them to realize we were involved because it would have complicated things for your parents. As far as they know, your parents really were just scientists who worked for Hi-Core Industries and not members of the FBI.

"If Herrington knew the full truth, I'm certain he would have killed them by now, with or without you in his custody. He's overly confident and thinks he'll simply buy his way through to you if anyone catches you. Your parents must be found quickly because soon Herrington won't care anymore if they live or die. Especially now that he knows we removed the ability for people to turn you in for the bounty."

"Do you know where my parents are?" Michael asked.

Daley cleared his throat. Michael thought he sounded uncomfortable.

"No, Michael, we don't know where they are," he said. "We know many of Herrington's hideouts, facilities, and bases of operations, but others keep springing up. If we don't find out some more information soon, we're going to have to risk intercepting Herrington's people searching for you and interrogate them. It'll most likely happen no later than tomorrow night."

If Daley was sharing, then it was his turn. Time for full disclosure. "Well, you better hurry because Danny thinks they're killing my dad."

Daley spoke slowly, carefully. "Why would he think that?"

"My dad showed up at the motel we stayed at the other night. He was a bird, and he was sitting outside our window. He was only there for a minute and then he disappeared, but Danny swears it was my father."

"Michael, hold on a minute," Daley said. Michael heard him put down the phone. In the background he heard Daley barking orders. There was a momentary discussion and then Daley got back on the phone. "You there, Michael?"

"Yeah, I'm here."

"Danny was certain it was your father?" he asked. "Not just another person who died?"

"No. Danny was sure it was him," he confirmed. "And, I am, too. The bird was looking right at us and then disappeared."

"It makes sense he would come to you if something happened to him. We figured your parents might be roughly interrogated, but not tortured to death."

"Do you think my Dad is dead?" he asked, quietly.

"Not if that bird really did disappear. If it truly was your father, then we need to find your parents immediately. I don't think he's dead yet, but he could be getting close."

Michael started to shake and begged his muscles to stay in control. "Danny thinks he's fighting a battle to stay alive. He says the bad men are hurting him enough to kill him. Mr. Daley, we have to find him." He glanced at his brother playing with the phone handset in the next booth. "Mr. Daley, how can Danny know all this?"

"It's no longer a question of how does he know this, but how much more does he know that he isn't letting on," Daley said. "Danny has a very powerful gift, an ability no one else has, and I believe when he said that bird was your father, it was. The decision is made, then. We don't have any more time to spare. We'll pick up one of Herrington's agents tonight. And we have to get you boys to safety. The people tracking you are actually close to your present location."

Michael gazed around the bowling alley worriedly. "How close are they?"

"Don't worry. About four hours away. They tracked the sedan you stole, but they'd been searching in the other direction and had to do an about-face. Great work back at the police station," he complimented. "You seem to have the makings of a first rate agent."

"No, thanks. As soon as this is all over, I'm never leaving my house again." Just then, he heard a strange clicking noise. He thought Mr. Daley might have been disconnected. "Hello, you still there, Mr. Daley?"

Daley's voice chimed in right away. "Yeah, I'm here. Why?"

"I thought I lost you for a second. There was a strange noise or something on my end."

Daley was immediately silent. Then Michael heard him ask someone to recheck the phone line to make sure no one was tapping in. After a few seconds he seemed to be satisfied and continued with what he was saying. "Okay, here's what we're going to do. I've got men in your area only an hour away. Until they get there I want you to go bowling."

"What? You want us to bowl?" Michael was incredulous. That was the last thing he wanted to do.

"Absolutely. It'll get your mind off what's happening to you for the moment, and it'll keep you safe and indoors. Normalcy, that's what we're looking for. Take your brother bowling and within the hour two plainclothes FBI agents will come for you."

"How will I know it's them?"

"I'll make sure one of them has an ice-cream cone for Danny. How's that?"

Michael was sure he could feel Daley smiling. "Okay, fine. And wait, just one more question before you go. Were you really watching out for me all these years?"

"Yes, a lot of us were, actually."

"Who else is involved?" Michael asked.

"Do you really want to know?" Daley asked. "It might make you feel like a fish in a glass tank to know who's been involved."

"Don't hold out on me, Mr. Daley. I already feel that way. After everything I've learned I just have to know the truth. I'm entitled to it."

"Of course, you are," he said, seriously. "Okay, there was Mr. Jacobs, your Scout Master, Danny's kindergarten teacher, Mrs. Smithey, Dobber, your pediatrician, Dr. Schwartz, and your next door neighbors, Mr. and Mrs. Polensky."

Michael gasped. "Dr. Schwartz and the Polenskys? But all of them are at least in their seventies."

Daley chuckled. "Don't let age fool you, Michael. Dr. Schwartz may look fragile, but it was all an act. As for the Polenskys, their job is simply to inform us of how you and your family go about your daily lives. They would be the ones who would report if anything out of the ordinary were happening. You might be interested to know they were the ones who got in touch with Dobber and told him to call and tell you to leave the house. The morning after the kidnapping."

"Incredible," Michael said.

"Trust me, Michael. We want to save your parents as much as you do. They're very fine people and an invaluable asset to our team. You should be proud of them—they really were winning an award at the Plaza. The fact of the matter is we screwed up. We should have known Herrington had caught on sooner to the phony documentation. There must have been a leak somewhere or else he just finally got his act in gear. But don't worry. We'll get to the bottom of this. We always do." He hung up.

Michael put the phone back and turned to Danny. "So, you want to go bowling?"

"I was hoping you'd let me," Danny signed, excitedly jumping up and down.

And for the next forty-five minutes, they bowled.

Chapter Fourteen

As Michael watched his brother bowl another gutter ball, he saw two men amble into the bowling alley. They both wore short-sleeve checkered shirts with jeans and jean jackets. One wore a Mets hat and the other sported a Yankees cap. Michael couldn't help laughing when he saw the one in the Yankees cap trying unsuccessfully to hold onto a swirl cone. He must have had it for a while because the ice cream was dripping down the sides of the cone, onto his hand.

"Hey, Danny," he signed. "Our new friends are here. They brought you an ice cream cone."

Danny jumped up, and they walked over to the agents.

The guy without the ice cream signed, "Hi, Danny and Michael. How are you guys?"

"You know sign language?" Danny asked, as he took the cone.

"Sure, doesn't everybody?" he spoke and signed simultaneously. Michael grinned at the strong southern twang and tried not to laugh at all the fresh nicks the agent had on his cheeks and chin, probably from shaving that morning.

To Michael, he turned and extended his hand. "My congratulations to you. You've done an outstanding job taking care of your brother and dealing with Herrington's agents. Totally embarrassed the guy, I'm sure. He's got billions at his discretion, and you guys keep slipping through his grasp. It's probably driving him crazy. Your parents will be very proud of you. I know Daley is." He pumped Michael's hand up and down.

"Thanks," he said, humbly.

"I'm Agent Porter, and this is my partner, Agent Cray." He flashed their badges. Agent Cray nodded and tipped his baseball hat with his dry hand. "We're going to take you guys to California where there's an FBI facility. You'll be safe there until we locate your parents."

After the agents paid for Michael and Danny's games and returned their shoes, they led them out to a rented gray Buick. "We're going to fly out of a small local airport, tickets and drinks compliments of the FBI." Agent Porter winked.

Michael liked this guy.

They climbed into the Buick. Agent Cray slid behind the wheel and drove them towards the highway. They were only on it for ten minutes when they turned off onto a side road. The drive took another twenty minutes. Agent Porter entertained them the entire time with stories from his training in the FBI. He even made some cracks about Daley in his training days, which Michael found hilarious. The fact he knew sign language made it all the more special because Danny could follow the entire conversation. Well, most of it.

Every once in a while Agent Porter did a two-handed sign that neither of them understood.

"I'm still learning," Agent Porter shrugged, sheepishly. "I have a daughter who's turning two and she was diagnosed as being hard of hearing earlier this year. I thought I should learn the language so we could communicate with her. Hard for this ol' Texas boy though," he said, tapping his forehead. "Thick skull."

"That's just what we did with Danny," Michael said. "Don't worry, you'll get the hang of it soon enough."

They finally drove up to a secluded airport. It was a small area cut into the side of a mountain. The expanse was about two hundred feet wide, five hundred feet long and bordered by craggy slopes, downed trees, and rocks. Agent Cray pulled up to a lone plane on the airstrip. It was what Michael's Mom would call a puddle-jumper. Michael couldn't believe this was what they were flying in. He'd expected something bigger.

Agent Porter saw his expression and laughed. "I know, it's not the biggest plane, but then again, it's not the smallest either and it's really nice inside. Leather seats, thirty-two inch flat screen TV, and loaded with snacks. We should be in California in just a few hours." He led them out of the car and onto the plane.

"Guys, we're going to go talk to the pilot back in the control room. It's over in that building," he said, pointing to what appeared to be a small concrete bunker about fifty feet away. "We'll be back in a little while. You know protocol," he said, rolling his eyes. "Feel free to make yourselves comfortable. The TV's over there and there's a bunch of videos as well, if you feel like watching. If you need anything, use the phone on the wall behind the seats. Just hit pound fifteen, and it'll go directly to my beeper."

As Agent Porter left the plane, Michael made himself comfortable on the plush seats. After a minute, he turned to Danny. His brother was scowling.

"Danny, you okay?"

He shook his head no and continued furrowing his brow as he stared out of the window.

He bent down to him. "What's the matter, Birdman? You can tell me," he signed, looking out the window as well. Both of the agents were still on the airstrip talking to someone whom Michael assumed to be the pilot. They were in a deep conversation and gesturing now and then at the plane.

Danny pointed towards a thick patch of grass off to the side of the plane. Michael saw a small gray mass within it, but he couldn't tell what it was.

"What is that?" Michael asked.

"Birds," Danny replied. "Dead birds."*

Danny turned to his brother, fear in his eyes. "I think these agents are the bad men. I think they killed those birds."

Michael stared at Danny, dumbstruck. No, this couldn't be happening again. Not when they were so close to safety. "Danny, why in the world would you think that?" He watched the men finish their discussion and move towards the control room.

"Because those birds haven't been dead long. I can tell. They never went to the light. I can see their old bodies just sitting there. Can't you see them? They're sitting on the grass, looking sad and all see-through. They're not going to be able to get to the light for a long time now and they know it." He turned to Michael, his eyes pleading with him. "It's really, really bad here. We have to leave."

"How many are there, Danny? How many birds do you see?"

Danny counted on his fingers. "Three. Two men and a lady."

Oh, my God. Could it be the two agents they were supposed to meet and the pilot? Was it possible? Could it be why Agent Porter signed words they didn't understand? Michael tried to make sense of it all. "Danny, can you tell who those birds were? Can you ask them any questions? Did Daley turn us in?" No! No! That couldn't be it.

Danny started crying. "I can't talk to them because they were killed in their bird bodies before I could speak to them. But, I know they were good people." He cried harder. "They killed them and now they're just sitting there. I can't help them. Michael, please, we have to get out of here before the bad men come back."

Michael knew he was out of his league on this one. After everything he'd been through and seen already, he trusted his brother's judgment entirely on this matter. It was the only explanation which made sense. Suddenly, another thought came to him. The clicking on the phone lines at the bowling alley. He was sure he remembered the first click came on exactly at the time Mr. Daley was explaining the plan to him. Herrington's people must have been listening. It wasn't Daley at all. Herrington's agents must have known about the airstrip and gotten agents to intercept them at the bowling alley.

"Danny, we're getting off the plane," he said, unbuckling their seat belts. Within seconds they were down the portable staircase. Luckily, the three people were still walking towards the control room and didn't see them drop to the ground and run around to the back of the plane.

"We've got to get to the car," he signed. They raced across the small tarmac and over to the Buick, hiding behind it. Michael peered into the front seat. No keys. Just his luck.

Danny tugged on his sleeve. Michael turned to him and followed Danny's pointed finger. He was directing his attention towards a place in the high grass. Michael's heart sank. If he had any more doubts at all, they were obliterated. There, in the brush, was a man's hand sticking out from between the rocks. It was covered with blood.

Danny signed frantically, "It's the good people. The bad people killed them and then killed them as birds so they wouldn't be able to help us or go to the light. Now they're going to kill us too, Michael." His whole body shook.

Michael grabbed his brother and hugged him hard, trying desperately to calm him down. "No one is going to kill us, Danny, I promise you, but we don't have much time. We've got to find a place to hide and the only one I can think of is over there by those people. There are a lot of rocks, and we can hide between them and try to escape up the mountain. Let's go." He pulled his brother towards the rocks, ducking the whole way. The ground sloped once they reached the rocks and Michael tried his best to drag Danny away from the dead bodies of the FBI agents. They slid down a small embankment and then hustled up and around some trees nestled against the side of the mountain. No sooner had they gotten behind the trees when the fake agents came out of the control room and started towards the plane.

"We've only got a few more minutes, Danny, please try to go faster." He pulled his brother into the trees. Soon, they were completely out of view of the airfield and surrounded by forest. Michael didn't know where they were running, but he knew they had to get as far away as possible. In the distance, he heard surprised shouts.

The sun was high in the sky and Michael couldn't make out which direction they were headed. They alternately walked and jogged, always making sure to keep on a straight path. Once again, running into nowhere.

Chapter Fifteen

Day 7 Sunday 1:00 p.m.

Michael checked his watch. They had been hiking through dense woods for almost two hours and were completely lost, covered with scratches from the brambles they'd constantly stumbled into, and filthy from head to toe. He smacked a mosquito off the back of his neck and tried not to listen to Danny whining he was hungry and thirsty. So was he.

Suddenly, he heard a noise ahead that tugged at his heart. Like the patter of rain on a roof, he recognized the tinkle of water rushing over rocks. Another minute of trekking brought them to a stream and they bent down greedily to drink from it.

"Don't fall in, Birdman," Michael said. "I don't have any clothes for you, and it's not warm out."

The stream led south, continuing down the mountain and they stuck with it, hoping it would eventually lead them to a small town. At least that's what he remembered from books about streams, always follow it to the end and you should find people.

Plopping himself on a log, Danny turned to his brother. "I want to go home."

Michael sat next to him. "Me, too. I promise it won't always be like this. We'll find the good people soon. They'll be able to take us to safety. We just need to keep on the run until we find them. It's like an adventure, isn't it?" He ruffled Danny's hair and brushed a mosquito off of his cheek.

Danny shook his head and frowned. "I don't like adventures anymore."

Michael sighed, agreeing with his brother whole-heartedly. "I don't like adventures anymore, either. I was just making a joke." He bent to get another handful of water from the stream, savoring its cool sweetness. Sitting here, surrounded by nothing but the forest, it was hard for him to believe so many bad things were happening in the world. One look at his brother's face, though, brought reality back into focus.

The kid was innocent, power or no power. He had never asked for this ability, and it was no one's right to try to take it away from him. He stood. "Come on, Danny. Let's go."

The stream eventually fed into a large lake nestled in a valley in the middle of the mountain. Surrounding the lake was an exclusive area of huge estates banked against it. As they ambled towards the first group of homes, Michael thought he heard a strange sound in the forest behind them. He froze, grabbing Danny. "Don't move," he signed.

After waiting for a few seconds, Michael didn't hear anything more and thought his nerves were just getting the best of him. Suddenly, it was there again. A light rustling, as if someone was moving stealthily through the forest.

"What's the matter?" Danny signed, looking around worriedly.

The rustling stopped again. Michael cocked his ear, straining to hear anything. All he heard was silence.

"I thought I heard something. I guess it was nothing." They started to walk again, with Michael occasionally glancing behind him to check the trees. Suddenly, he saw two men come into view, about three hundred yards behind them. It was Agent Porter and Agent Cray, and they were running full speed towards them, brandishing guns.

Michael was in a panic. "It's the bad agents. Danny, run." They raced as fast as they could around the lake.

The men were gaining and yelling for Michael to stop. They said some more things, but Michael's adrenaline was racing so fast and his heart was pounding so loudly he couldn't hear what they were saying. Nor did he want to. All he wanted to do was get as far away from them as possible. It was going to be close. Danny stumbled, and Michael swooped him into his arms and pounded around the first house they came to. It was a modern, art deco style home of light-colored wood and glass, with large windows which faced the lake. They had to run past the private pier and up onto the tiled driveway. When they neared the front of the house, Michael sought a hiding place and saw an open garage door in the house next door. Jumping over some low hedges, he rushed over to it and pulled Danny inside, finally ducking behind the black BMW parked there.

As Michael peeked around the car he saw the two phony agents come tearing into view. They no longer looked like the kind men who had picked them up back at the bowling alley.

The men approached the first house and rang the doorbell. No one answered. They tried the door, but it was locked. Michael watched as Agent Cray aimed his gun and shot at the door jamb. It splintered apart and the agents kicked in the door. They stormed into the house.

Suddenly, Michael heard a commotion near them.

"Hey, what the hell?" an elderly voice shouted from inside the house where they hid.

"Marv, what's going on? Did the Hellerman's Mercedes backfire again?"

The front door opened.

Michael peeked around the car and saw the man's face. He seemed alarmed. "No, I don't think it was their car, hon. Do me a favor and stay inside, will ya?" He closed the front door and went back into the house.

He emerged less than a minute later with a rifle in his hands and a frantic woman attached to his arm.

"Esther, listen to me, woman," he barked. "Get inside and call 911. Do it now." His wife whimpered and ran back into the house.

Just as she ran inside, Cray and Porter stormed out of the Hellerman's house. They stopped when they saw Marv with his gun pointed at them. He had moved down the steps and now stood in front of his open garage.

Porter flashed an I.D. badge. "Hello, sir. No need to point that thing at us. We're the good guys. Agents from the FBI. Why don't you put the gun away before someone gets hurt?" He was playing his southern accent to the max.

Marv chuckled sarcastically. "Oh, really now? Didn't know FBI agents made a habit of shooting their way into innocent people's homes while they're away on vacation— except in the movies, that is." He kept the gun trained on them.

Porter started to walk towards the house. "Sir, this is a top secret government investigation involving traitors to the United States. We think their children have escaped to this area. We've been told they're armed and dangerous."

"I think that'll be your last step, Agent," Marv said coolly. "I may be an old man, but I'm an excellent shot and have no problem shooting at anyone who comes onto my property uninvited. You might be interested to know I'm also a former Navy SEAL and know all about protocol. As for the kidnapped American scientists I believe you're referring to, I recall the government just announced they were neither spies nor terrorists. As for their children, I personally don't see how a seventeen-year-old and a six-year-old could be much of a threat to you."

Porter raised his voice menacingly. "You're obstructing justice, sir. Now, if you don't put that gun down right now, we will charge you with a federal offense."

"I'd like to see you try." The men stared at each other, waiting for the moment either one or the other would give in.

Unaware of what was going on, Esther came bolting out the front door. "Marv, I called 911, they're com...," It was all she got out before Cray drew his gun, lightning fast, and shot Esther. She screamed once and fell to the floor. As her husband stared at his wife's body, Porter immediately took advantage of the situation and took aim. This time the shot was directed at Marv.

Marv reacted in the nick of time and moved so he only took the brunt of the bullet in his left shoulder. The force of the bullet drove him backwards into the garage.

Marv still had his rifle clutched in his right hand and held on to it tightly as he dragged himself behind his car.

Safely hidden for the moment he glanced to his right and gasped, half in surprise and half in pain, when he saw Michael and Danny crouching next to him.

Michael crawled over to him, speaking urgently. "It's us they're after. Please, what can I do to help?"

Marv slumped back against the wall, grimacing in pain. "Where are they now?"

Michael glanced under the car and saw the agents inching tentatively towards the open garage. "They're coming towards us," he whispered.

Marv nodded, his face decisive. "Do you know how to fire one of these?" he asked, breathing heavily. Blood ran down his shirt, and he was starting to sweat.

"No," Michael said, his heart pumping so hard he thought it would explode. He knew what the man wanted him to do.

"Well, then you better learn fast," Marv said. "Take the gun and balance it on your shoulder. Look through that little piece there. That'll help you line up your target. And then pull the trigger and kill those bastards. The safety's off. All you have to do is get the image as close as possible to your target. The bullet will do the rest. Do it now before they come any closer or there won't be another chance. Do it now."

Michael was terrified he would screw up and get them all killed, but he had no choice. There was no one else capable of doing what had to be done. Sweating, he hoisted the gun up onto his shoulder and stood. Immediately, Porter took a shot at him. The bullet flew right by Michael's left ear and he flinched as pieces from the garage wall behind him sprayed his back from the force of the gunshot. Before Porter could fire another shot, Michael pulled the trigger. The report was so loud his ears rang and the kick was so fierce it threw him back against the side wall of the garage. He slumped to the floor, holding his shoulder.

Groaning, Marv leaned over and peeked under the car. He nodded. "Not bad. Not bad at all."

Michael dared to take a peek, but wished he hadn't. Porter lay on the ground, the upper half of his body a ruined mess. Cray was nowhere to be seen.

"Is he dead?" Michael asked, his voice shaking.

"Oh, I'd say so," Marv replied, resting back against the wall. "Dirty bastard deserved it."

Revulsion filled Michael's chest and he was overcome. He turned to the back wall and threw up. After a few more dry heaves he was finally able to calm down and turned to Marv who stared at him.

"Never killed a man before, have you?" he wheezed.

"No. Guess there's always a first time," Michael said weakly, wiping his mouth. He glanced at his brother, nearly forgetting he was there. Danny sat on the floor terrified, curled into a ball. There was no time to comfort him.

Marv was speaking to him. "Hey, kid? Remember, we still got another one of those killers out there. Now get that gun in your hands again. I'm too weak to help you. I take it you're the kids of Herrington's spies?"

"We're not spies," Michael mumbled.

"Don't worry. I don't care who or what the hell you are. All I care about is killing those men who shot my Esther. If you want to protect this little brother of yours, I suggest you get up now and nail the second guy. I doubt he'll treat you or your brother very kindly if he has the opportunity to catch up with you." Beads of sweat bloomed on his face and his breathing became shallower.

His comment about Danny moved Michael to action. He pushed himself up and was going to walk out of the garage to confront the agent when he heard Danny cry out "Mi Mi." That was Danny's call for his brother, to catch his attention when Michael wasn't looking at him.

Michael turned to see Danny pointing to the closed door leading from inside the garage to the house. Two feet in brown hiking boots were showing underneath the crack between the door and the floor.

"Anyone in your house other than you and your wife?" Michael asked Marv.

Marv shook his head no. "Do it."

Michael took one deep breath, aimed the gun and after bracing for the recoil, he fired into the door. It blasted apart, and Cray, wide-eyed, flew backwards into the kitchen, a hole the size of a softball ripping through his stomach.

Michael dropped the gun and sat heavily on the garage floor, numb and in shock. He remained that way, hugging his knees and shaking while Danny went to him and grabbed tightly onto his arm. It was all Michael could do to get one arm around his brother. But once he did, he grabbed Danny in a huge bear hug, not letting go until the police cars from the 911 call finally arrived.

Chapter Sixteen

Day 7 Sunday 8:00 p.m.

Kentrall Memorial Hospital

"Michael, there you are," Daley called, flashing his badge as he stormed into the emergency room. Michael glanced up and smiled weakly at him, holding an icepack to his bruised shoulder.

"Thank God. How you doing, kid?" With his disheveled hair and dark circles under his eyes, Daley looked as if had run fifteen miles straight just to get to him.

"I'm doing okay, I guess," Michael said, quietly. "You know I killed them, Mr. Daley. I killed the guys who were after my brother."

"I heard, Michael," he said. "I contacted the local police as soon as our agents didn't call into our field office to report a successful contact with you. I got on a plane immediately." He ran his hands through his thinning hair. "I'm so sorry this happened. We couldn't believe we screwed up again, so we retraced the phone lines and learned of the tap. It's by far the most sophisticated tapping system we've ever encountered. Years beyond anything we've developed, but it doesn't excuse anything. I'm horrendously embarrassed. This is our fault and our fault alone. I can't begin to apologize for what you just went through and have been going through."

Michael could see the pain in his teacher's eyes. He really did care. "It's okay. I'm just glad you're here."

"I'm not going to leave you or your brother alone again. Our people will always be with you until this thing is solved. You did the right thing with those killers, Michael. You had no choice, and no one could've done it better. I'm serious. You did great."

Michael brushed aside the compliment. It just didn't seem right he should be praised for killing someone, even considering the circumstances involved. Instead of feeling relieved and proud, he felt sick to his stomach. He shuddered and closed his eyes. Now he knew how all those soldiers felt when the army thrust guns into their hands and told them to go kill some people in towns across the world. Now he was just like them.

Daley put a comforting hand on his good shoulder. "If this helps, from what Marvin Levy told the police, you're a hero. You acted like a pro, listened to his directions under severe pressure, and didn't freeze up. If you had, Herrington's agents would have surely killed Marvin and his wife, and taken Danny. You stopped them. That—and only that—is what you have to remember."

Michael glanced up, surprised. "Marv's wife is alive?"

Daley smiled. "She's a very lucky woman. Just got out of surgery about a half an hour ago. Took a bullet in her chest, which missed her heart by only a fraction of an inch. She's expected to make a complete recovery in a few weeks' time."

"And Marv? Is he okay?"

"He'll be just fine. Took the bullet in his shoulder. It went straight through. A few painkillers, some stitches, and he was as good as new." He chuckled. "Ever since Marv found out Ester was all right, he's been talking up a storm about his time in the military. Tough as nails, that guy." He glanced at the next bed. "How's the little one doing?"

They peered at the jumble of white blankets curled into a tight ball on the bed next to them. Tufts of dark brown hair escaped onto the pillow.

"He's finally asleep. The doctor gave him a light sedative because his heartbeat was soaring so high," Michael said. "Danny wouldn't let go of my leg and they wanted to check out my shoulder, so the doctor thought it would be best if he got some rest."

Daley turned to him. "And you? How are you doing, really?"

"I'll be okay, I guess. What I really want to do now is just find my parents and end this. Are there any leads, yet? Any at all?"

"We just picked up one of Herrington's agents. He's now in custody in our field office in Southern California and being questioned as we speak."

Michael was quiet for a moment, but then asked the question that was burning in his mind. "Do you think my parents are still alive?"

Daley looked him straight in the eye. "I know they are."

He searched for any lie in Mr. Daley's face, but didn't see one. "How can you be so sure?"

"I'm sure because if they had died, they would have come to you as birds. They would have stayed with you until they knew you were safe."

Michael breathed a sigh of relief, realizing that was exactly what would have happened. "Of course. And if they were killed, I think Danny would have known somehow."

A few members of Daley's staff completed the necessary paperwork to release them. Then, the agents gently picked up Danny, who was still fast asleep, and carried him out to the car. Michael followed behind with Daley.

"Want to ride up front, Michael?" Daley asked.

"No. I'd like to sit back here with Danny if that's okay with you."

"It's fine."

This time they drove to a much larger airport and were booked on a charter plane to the FBI's field office in Southern California. Once the car reached the airport, Danny woke up. He immediately started to cry and grabbed for Michael. Michael held him until he calmed and then pointed to Mr. Daley who had turned around and was smiling and waving from the front seat. In fact, Daley was making all sorts of funny faces and expressions to get Danny to laugh.

Danny stared at him cautiously for a few minutes and then cracked a smile. One became two and soon he was laughing in the backseat.

Michael reveled in how a six-year-old could go from totally disoriented one minute, to completely comfortable the next. It wasn't hard to understand why, though. That was the kind of kid Danny was. He knew those men had been dangerous and were partly responsible for what was happening to his family. He seemed to have a different perspective of life and death than most people, knowing that bad people really did get punished in the end.

Danny also trusted him and if he told his brother everything was okay, then it was. As only a six-year-old could, Danny put the events at Marv's house behind him and immersed himself with the planes on the airstrip.

Approximately thirty minutes later they cleared airport security and were seated in the luxury cabin of a Boeing 747. It was the most incredible plane Michael had ever seen. It was set up like a living room with cream-colored leather seats, couches, and wooden tables. There was a whole computer area with top of the line equipment, and there were flowers everywhere.

"Like the accommodations, boys?" Daley asked.

Michael nodded. Daley leaned in and whispered close to Michael's ear. "You know, the president and his family have used this plane. In fact, you're sitting in the very seat he likes to sit in. So, sit back and enjoy the ride."

The plane was staffed with two pilots and two stewards, all of whom were employed by the FBI. Michael felt like royalty when the steward asked him for a pre-takeoff drink and was ecstatic when they suggested Danny go up front to meet the pilots. Michael had not seen Danny this happy in the last week. As the plane taxied down the runway, Michael settled back in his chair and quickly fell asleep. It was Monday, 2:25 a.m.

Chapter Seventeen

Day 8 Monday 3:25 a.m.

On an isolated island one mile off the shore of a small village town in Southern California

"Gary, can you hear me?" Maddy whispered. "Please answer me if you can." His head was in her lap and she gently stroked his face, trying to wake him up. After Herrington's people had beaten him again, he had lost consciousness for the fourth time. Disgusted, they tossed him in one of the old storerooms. When they couldn't obtain any more information from Maddy, they threw her in with him and locked the door. That was two hours ago, and she still couldn't get Gary to wake up.

She pleaded with him, trying desperately not to cry, trying not to see the permanent damage the savages had inflicted on him from the poisons they had leaked into his system. "Honey, I'm here. Everything's going to be okay. I just need you to wake up, all right?" She had been crying for days and was all out of tears. No matter how efficient her training had been at the FBI, they couldn't erase her emotions. Watching her husband being tortured and knowing her sons were in danger had terrorized her to no end. But she knew remaining silent, only pretending she would give them the information they needed, and maintaining her alias—those were the things keeping her and Gary alive. They would have to kill her before she would do anything to put her children in jeopardy. Just then Gary moaned.

"That's it, wake up and come back to me."

Gary finally came to, groggy and confused.

"Maddy, that you?" he croaked. His voice was raspy and weak, and Maddy strained to hear him.

"Yes, it's me," she said.

He tried to sit up and fell on her shoulders. She cradled him in her arms.

He grabbed at her arms weakly, desperate to talk to her. "I've seen them. I've seen the boys. They're okay, or were when I saw them a few days ago."

She desperately wanted to believe him, but knew it was impossible. "You must have been dreaming, honey."

"No, I wasn't. After I passed out in the interrogation room, I left my body and saw them. I just haven't had a chance to tell you." His words came out slowly, haltingly.

She stared at him, gulping back her fear. If Gary had truly seen them, he had been close enough to death to travel to their children. She didn't know how much more abuse he would be able to take and survive.

She tried to hide her concern, to put the hope back in her voice so her fear wouldn't betray her. "Gary, tell me more, sweetie. Where were they? Was anyone with them?"

"No, they were alone. It was wild, Maddy. There was a white light above me, so brilliant and powerful, and next to me in every direction were miles and miles of birds. The light drew me in and gave me such comfort. There was no pain, no fear. But I wasn't ready to leave, no matter how beautiful the light felt. I pulled away from it and felt my soul fly into one of the birds. As soon as I connected, I traveled straight to Danny." He paused, catching his breath. "He's like a beacon. You just see him and feel him—you're drawn to him. I flew right to a windowsill outside of a hotel, and as I sat there, deciding what to do next, Michael pulled aside the curtain, and both of them were staring directly at me. I tried to speak to them, to Danny, when suddenly I was pulled away and woke up, back in the interrogation room. I could read Danny's mind for that instant. They've been running from Herrington's agents. I could tell a few times it had been close, but Michael had gotten them away. They don't have them yet, Maddy."

Maddy closed her eyes and was so proud of her eldest son she couldn't even speak. Neither of them had ever told Michael anything about their pasts because they didn't want him to be used as a pawn for any government or organization. They were so sure their covers would never be blown, that they would never be discovered. It had been a terrible mistake. She had put him in jeopardy. She could just imagine what he thought of them.

She sighed. "We should have told Michael about Danny. We shouldn't have kept it a secret."

"He knows about Danny," he said. "At least, now he does. I could see in his eyes he knew. Maddy, I have to go back and find them."

She turned to him, horrified. "You can't mean that. You almost died on me. That's why you were able to find the boys in the first place. If you try to get back there, you might never make it back to your body."

"You know I have to," he pleaded with her. "No one has any idea where we are, and I have to try to get word out of our location. We don't have a lot of time left. If I can do anything to protect you, I will."

"No, I won't let you risk your life for me. As long as I know my boys are safe, I can live with the consequences. I can't let you die for me. I couldn't live with that. Please, I'm begging you not to go again."

"Look, we're not going to be able to resist much longer. If we don't do something now, Herrington is going to kill the both of us and then the boys will have no one. This is our only chance." He paused. "I don't have to die."

She was confused. "What do you mean? You're going to be as close to death as you can get. How else can it be done?"

"I think I can connect to Danny when I'm unconscious, just like the last time. I remember leaving my body for a moment, almost like when you're just about to fall asleep.

You're half in and half out of consciousness, and then suddenly you're completely aware and alive, but in a special dream phase."

Maddy's eyes widened. "So you believe when we're rendered unconscious because of an accident or a severe head injury, it's as if the body is trying to decide if it's going to continue to live or not? Maybe that's the reason people always say they see a white light in a life or death situation and are drawn to it. Maybe they simply can't resist the pull and just let it take them away."

Gary nodded. "But I won't let that happen. I think if I provoke them again and they beat me, I can go back to that state and find the boys and tell them where we are."

"But what if you can't find them? And then what if you can't find your way back to me? The alternative is intolerable. You'll be dead."

"I'll find my way back to you, Maddy," he said. "I told you, Danny is like a beacon in this semi-conscious phase. There's an aura around him, lighting him up. I can feel my soul actually seeking him out. He's truly beautiful."

"His power's that strong?"

"It's the strongest thing I've ever experienced. Our research never prepared us for the reality of what this boy can truly do. Trust me, I can do this. It's the only way."

They heard footsteps trudging down the corridor towards their cell. Wincing, Gary raised his head and kissed his wife. "I love you, Maddy. With all my heart."

Herrington and the interrogator came into the room.

Gary called out to him, mockingly. "What's the matter? Things not looking up for Marta?"

His eyes bulging in anger, Herrington reared back and punched Gary in the face.

Maddy would swear later Gary smiled as he blacked out.

Chapter Eighteen

Day 8 Monday 3:25 a.m.

In the air

Danny bolted up in his chair. "Daa," he cried out.

"Danny, what is it?" Michael asked. "What's the matter?"

"Daa," he said again. Then he signed "Daddy" and glanced at Michael worriedly.

At the same moment, one of the pilots called for Daley over the intercom. "Could you please come up front, sir?"

Daley glanced at Danny curiously and then went into the control room. The intercom was still on, and Michael could hear the entire conversation.

"What's going on, Captain?" Daley asked.

"Sir, we're flying at an altitude of 25,000 feet and for the past five minutes we keep noticing a bird popping up around the plane," he said. "I can't explain it, sir."

Daley's voice sounded sarcastic. "You see a bird up this high? In the dark?"

"That's affirmative. I know this sounds unbelievable, but it keeps appearing and disappearing. Hey, there it is again. Man, that's one huge bird, like eight or nine feet with the wingspan." Michael could hear the awe in the pilot's voice.

"Never seen anything like it," the copilot said. "It's like it's looking right at us. Wait, it's gone again. See what we mean?"

"Keep this speed and maintain it until you hear further instructions," Daley said.

Michael heard movement and then saw Daley striding through the cabin.

Danny had been staring intently out the window and Daley shook his arm to get his attention. Then he turned to Michael. "Sign for me. I need to ask him something."

"Danny," he said, "the pilots keep seeing a bird outside of the plane. Do you know anything about this?"

Danny stared at Michael wide-eyed and nodded.

"Who is it?"

"Is it a condor, Mr. Daley?" Michael asked. "The California Condor on the endangered species list?"

Daley didn't seem surprised by the question. "It's your dad, isn't it?"

Danny nodded, "Me Daa." Danny started to sign quickly and Michael had to hurry to interpret. "He says it's our Dad, but the plane is too high up here for him to stay as a real bird. There's not enough oxygen, and it's too cold. If he stays, he'll freeze in his bird body. He needs to meet us on the ground, where it's warmer. Right now, he's just a vision."

Daley called over one of his officers. "Call Air Traffic Control and alert them that we need to drop to a lower altitude for the remainder of the trip, preferably ten thousand feet or less. I'll explain later."

The officer ran to the cockpit. Within seconds their ears popped and they felt the plane descend.

"Do you know how long before we land?" he asked another officer.

"About an hour, give or take, sir."

Daley turned to Danny. "What does this mean, Danny? Does this mean your father has died?"

Danny shrugged his shoulders, frustrated. "I don't know. It's not like the others. All the other birds are surrounded by a light that always tries to draw them away from me. Daddy's light isn't strong at all. It's like he's not real, like he shouldn't be here. It's like he's a fake bird or something."

"Danny, do you think Dad might just be trying to get to us somehow?" Michael asked. "To help us?"

Danny shrugged again. "I don't know."

"Do you think he's dead?" Michael signed, afraid to know the answer, but too scared not to ask.

Danny started to cry and slammed his hands on the seat, rocking in frustration. "I don't know. I don't know. It's not like the others. He won't come to me because we're too high up. I don't understand."

"It's okay, Danny. It's okay," Michael soothed, glancing at Mr. Daley worriedly. "Once we get on the ground, we'll see if we can find Dad. He'll tell us what to do next."

So, they sat for the next hour, waiting expectantly and nervously for what they would be met with on the airstrip. The pilots didn't see the Condor again until they landed.

Chapter Nineteen

Day 8 Monday 4:25 a.m.

A private airport in California

The plane touched ground, and as soon as it landed Danny and Michael unhooked their seatbelts and ran to the front of the aircraft. Once the doors were unlocked and the steps installed, they raced down and stood on the tarmac, the lights on, searching around desperately for any sign of the condor.

They were met by an entire entourage of no less than fifty FBI agents and security vehicles, waiting to whisk them to safety.

"Michael, do you see him?" Daley asked, coming up behind them.

"No, not yet." Suddenly, out of nowhere the condor appeared and flew directly at Danny. It landed next to him. Danny dropped to his knees and bear hugged the enormous creature.

Michael started to cry when he saw the bird gently rub its beak into Danny's hair. The condor cawed once, signaling Danny to let it go and it hopped over to Michael. Michael bent to its eye level, wiping the tears from his eyes. "Hi, Dad."

The condor cawed twice and spread its wings.

Daley came over and bent down to the condor, staring in awe. He asked Michael to translate. "Can your dad take us to him and your mother?"

The condor faced Daley and flapped his wings.

Daley's smile widened. "Well, I'll be damned. Gary, I need to ask you some questions."

The condor closed its eyes for a moment and then Danny started signing while Michael translated. "Danny says you can talk to my father and he'll translate for us. It'll be quicker. Go ahead, Mr. Daley. Ask your questions."

Daley took a deep breath. "Are you dead?"

Danny shook his head no.

"Then how is this happening?"

Danny stared at his dad for a long time before finally breaking into a huge smile. "He tricked them. He's not dead, just unconscious. He made Mr. Herrington hit him over the head to knock him out and he figured he could jump into a bird body that way. Oh, I understand now, Daddy."

"Where's Mom?" Michael asked, worriedly. "Is she okay?"

"For now, but she's running out of time. She hasn't given Herrington the information he wants—where you both are, how the machine was built, the location of the documents substantiating our research, and he's going to start on her next. Daley, he's poisoning us, using his serums. You have to get to us soon or I don't think we'll make it." He paused. "He's getting desperate and knows the FBI is involved."

"Do you know your location?" Daley asked.

Danny continued translating. "I think we're near the ocean. We took a plane, then cars and then felt like we were on a boat at one point. I can smell the salt in the air. I think you're close, too. I feel much stronger here in this body than I did when I first came to the kids once before. It's as if I'm not drawing my energy from far away. If it's any help, I could also detect the sound of mice and the caws of owls. The last time I heard that was years ago when Maddy and I first met Herrington. He'd taken us to one of his islands and this particular one always had a huge problem with mice."

Daley thought for a moment, his eyes widening. "I think I may know where you are. Just hold on a little longer." Daley flipped open his cell phone and barked orders into it.

Danny moved over to Michael. "Daddy says he's very proud of you."

Michael choked up. "Thanks, Dad."

Suddenly, Danny ran to the condor and started signing frantically. "What's the matter? Daddy, don't go."

The condor started to jerk, turning in frantic circles.

"Dad, no," Michael shouted. "Don't go yet."

He tried to grab on to his father but no sooner did he get to him, then the condor collapsed to the ground. A dark shadow streaked from the bird, racing across the tarmac.

"Danny, where did he go?" Michael cried. "Why did he leave?"

"Herrington's waking him up," he said. "He thinks they're on to him."

Chapter Twenty

Day 8 Monday 5:00 a.m.

Island facility off of California

"Wake him." Herrington stormed into the room with his guards.

"Leave him alone," Maddy cried out. "Haven't you done enough?" She ran to protect Gary, who lay unconscious on the floor. Herrington struck her in the face, sending her sprawling across the room where she hit the wall.

She slid onto the floor, holding her bloody lip and watched helplessly while the guards lifted Gary into a chair and began working on him. One of the guards shoved smelling salts under his nose. When that didn't wake him they took out a syringe filled with a cloudy liquid and slid the needle into his arm. Seconds later, he opened his eyes, gasping.

Herrington put his face close to Gary's. "I'm on to you. You think I'm going to let you die so you can contact the police and bring them here? Do you think I'm that stupid? You're no good to me dead, yet." He moved over to Maddy, hauling her to her feet, then began pacing the room, his insane gaze darting back and forth between their faces. "I propose a bargain, just like I do with governments around the globe who don't want to play nice. I have something you want and you have something I want. Let's make a trade."

"What could you possibly have that we want?" Maddy spit out.

"I have your sons," Herrington said.

Maddy gasped and glanced at Gary, but his expression never wavered.

"I'll give you both your freedom and your sons if you promise to share everything you've learned," he said. "Tell me the truth about the machine, not the lies you've been spouting, and I'll bring them right to you."

"You have my boys?" Gary asked, his voice weak. "Where are they? Bring them here to me now, and I'll tell you anything you want to know about the machine."

"Gary, no," Maddy shouted. "He can't be trusted."

"If you have them, bring them here," Gary demanded, ignoring her.

Herrington fidgeted slightly.

Gary smiled and closed his eyes. "You're lying. You don't have them. This is all because of Marta, you despicable man. She's dying from one of your own damned viruses you allowed to get out of control and now you're prepared to kill everyone in your efforts to save her soul. Well, guess what, Samuel? She's damned and nothing you can do, nothing you learn, will save her. She wrote her own death sentence before you even met her. Once she married you, she cemented it in stone. There won't be any afterlife for her, no matter how much money you have."

Herrington flew over to him and violently pushed Gary off his chair and onto the floor, and then he grabbed him, shoving his face in his. "Tell me where the damned machine is."

"No," Gary said. He turned his eyes to Maddy, sadness in them, but his face resolute. "The answer is no."

Herrington stilled, realizing Gary was prepared to die. He eyed Maddy. "I only need one of you." He motioned to his guards. Herrington turned to glance back before he shut the door and made one final comment. "Gary, you have until eight a.m. to tell me what I need to know. That's in three hours. After that, you're dead. You can then contact whomever you want, but know you'll be leaving your wife to take your place in that chair with a host of different cocktails I'll personally put together to give her the maximum amount of pain and suffering. The choice is yours." He slammed the door behind him.

Maddy ran over to Gary, smothering him in kisses. "Oh, I'm so glad you're back."

"I told you I'd come back," he whispered.

"I know. How can you be so sure that he doesn't have the boys?"

His expression said it all, and her eyes widened. "It worked, didn't it? You saw them again, didn't you?"

Gary nodded, wincing. "And they're okay. They're with Bob Daley and his staff, nearby. I told them as much as I could. I think they'll be able to find us. We just have to hold out a little bit longer." He gripped her tightly.

"Can you hold out?"

"I'll try." He closed his eyes and rested his head in her lap.

They had three hours.

Chapter Twenty-One

Michael couldn't believe his dad was gone. To have him so close for just a moment! He glanced at the inert condor on the ground and then at Daley, who continued to fire orders into his cell phone.

"Yes, that's what I said," Daley said. "Islands, pharmaceutical facilities, anything ever listed to Herrington. Look back in the files, see any place Gary and Maddy have lived or worked after they were contacted by Herrington. Call me at this number as soon as you have something." He closed the phone. "We're going to our field office, about twenty miles east of here. An old friend is going to take you boys there."

A tall, burly man with close cropped, blond hair and ruddy cheeks ambled over to them. "Hey, Michael. How you doing?"

Michael's eyes widened. "Dobber!"

The agent smiled. "Though now I'm Secret Agent Dobber and not Mr. Scientist man. I can't tell you how sorry I am about everything that's happened, but you've amazed me. The way you've acted and conducted yourself is incredible."

Dobber nodded at Danny, signing hello and Danny broke into a smile and ran over to him, hugging his huge legs.

225

"Come, boys, your car is waiting," Dobber said. He brought them over to a stretch black limo. "We've got a lot of homework to catch up on, Danny," he signed, as they climbed in. The car started, and Dobber put the privacy panel up.

Michael sat back and caught sight of a black box lying in the middle of the limo floor. It was exactly like the one he'd seen in the pictures back in the sedan. He got onto the floor and peered at the box. "Is this what I think it is? Is this the famous machine?"

"Yep," Dobber replied. "Your parents made me promise if anything were to happen to them, I was to continue working with Danny to get him up to level fifteen. We weren't to waste any time because if they were ever in trouble, then it meant their cover had been blown." He turned to Danny. "You need to be able to protect yourself, so we have to make sure your abilities are as high as they can go, so no one can ever hurt you. You understand?"

Danny nodded.

"Good," he said. "They gave me the code word, bluebeard, so you would know I was one of the good guys. Do you remember your mommy telling you that?"

Danny nodded again. "She told it to me every night before I went to bed."

"That's right," Dobber said. "Even though you and I know each other and are friends, she wanted to make sure you knew it was okay to work with me without her around. Do you want to begin?"

Michael saw Danny nod and became concerned. "Wait. You're going to work with him on the machine now? You're going to experiment on my brother right in front of me?" He couldn't believe this. Did the madness never end?

Dobber shook his head. "Michael, I'm not going to do anything but guide him if he needs it. Danny can do this all on his own."

With that, Danny got down on the floor next to the box, as the limo made its way out of the airport. He glanced at Dobber. "Where are the ears?"

"Do you mean the headset?"

Danny nodded.

"You don't need to wear them," Dobber explained. "Your mom only used them to help you concentrate. Now, just try to focus your thoughts and concentrate on the lights. Soon, you'll be so strong you won't even need the machine. Here, let's start at level one." He flicked on the first dial and the first light came on. "You've already made it as far as level thirteen, but it's been almost a week since you've practiced, so let's take it slow and see how far you can go."

He turned to Michael. "Sit back and brace yourself, Michael, because you're in for quite a ride. Just be still and take it in, but above all, don't be alarmed or try to stop what happens. This is your brother's show, and he's completely safe."

Michael moved off the floor and sat back on the seat, apprehensively.

When Dobber was ready, he turned to Danny. "Go ahead, Danny, it's all yours."

Danny closed his eyes and his brows creased in concentration. Like a psychic at a séance, he seemed to go into a deep trance, as if channeling a spirit from a far off world. The hyper little boy, who couldn't sit still for more than a few seconds at a time, was silent and thoughtful, concentrating on the task at hand.

Michael's ears suddenly popped and while he stretched his mouth around to try to regain the equilibrium, a soft humming noise seemed to emanate from the walls of the car. It increased little by little until it became a steady pulse all around him. One by one, the light bulbs on the machine turned on, though no one was touching them. Two, three, four. With the turning on of each light, the humming became increasingly stronger and louder. It seemed to spring from everywhere and nowhere at the same time as if hidden speakers were turned on throughout the walls of the car.

When the fifth light appeared, the humming changed. Michael was sure he could discern the flapping of birds' wings fluttering all around him. He glanced at Dobber, who appeared to have no reaction to what was happening, his concentration centered solely on Danny.

Michael turned to peer out the windows, trying to see where they were driving to, but the windows had fogged up. Putting his hand up to wipe off the condensation, he flinched as something rubbed against his leg. He bent to see what was there, then something light and feathery brushed his cheek. He had sensations all over his body of things crawling on him, as if he had jumped into the middle of an ant farm. Trying to brush off the invisible bugs, he called to Dobber and Danny, but neither answered him. In fact, it seemed they were completely oblivious as to what was happening to him.

How could that be? Why weren't either of them fazed by what was going on? The humming grew louder now and started to hurt his ears. He searched desperately for the source, but he couldn't pinpoint it. Then he felt another sensation on his left arm, harder this time, coaxing him with a teasing caress. He glanced quickly to his left, smacking his arm, but again, there was nothing.

Michael gaped as the sixth, seventh and eighth lights flicked on effortlessly. His brother remained completely relaxed and still as a stone statue, his eyes closed. When the eighth light brightened, Michael involuntarily clenched his fists shut as shadows flickered in and out of his vision. Squeezing his eyes closed, he wanted to cry out, to make the images and the onslaught stop, but he knew he wouldn't. This was what Herrington wanted from his brother and no matter how scared and confused he was by what was happening, he was damned if he wasn't going to learn all there was to know about Danny's powers. If his brother could go through this unaffected, then he could, too. Trying to regain his composure, Michael forced himself to open his eyes and was greeted with a multitude of impossible shadows. Shadows of hundreds of birds flying around inside the car.

Sweat dripped off his forehead and he wiped his brow, his hand glistening as if he had just come out of a pool. The car was getting hotter by the minute. Condensation dribbled in rivulets from the windows like melting snow. Michael glimpsed his brother through the shadows and saw him raise his hands high and tilt his head back to the ceiling. He resembled a holy man asking the sky-god for rain.

Michael couldn't keep quiet any longer. "What's he doing?" he yelled to Dobber, straining to be heard above the tumult.

Dobber put a finger to his lips and shook his head.

This was unbearable. The humming grated up and down his spine and the invisible pokes and prods were unnerving. "Dobber," he pleaded. "I have to know what's going on."

"Just watch," Dobber said. "Watch and you'll see. It's coming any minute."

Unbelievably the noise level increased, as if ten thousand people had decided to speak at once. Then twenty thousand—

a hundred thousand. Michael screamed and brought his hands to his ears to drown out the clamor. He stared, frightened, as the ninth, tenth, and eleventh lights turned on. He tasted blood and forced himself to stop biting his bottom lip. His heart raced with anticipation of what each new light would bring. It didn't take long to find out. With each one, the shadows took on more life. The birds were becoming solid, their numbers doubling and tripling in size. Their screeching and cawing joined the cacophony already in the car until Michael could no longer hear himself scream.

Finally, the twelfth and thirteenth lights lit up. The birds were alive and all around him, hundreds flying inside of the car, like the maelstrom of a cycling tornado. Even though he knew it was impossible for the car to hold so many there seemed to be enough room, as if the area within the car had actually grown larger.

The birds continued to fly in circles around his head and a sense of recklessness came over him. He put aside his fear and cautiously reached his hand out to touch one of the images, but instead of touching feathers, his hand went right through it. Amazed, he tried again. His hand sliced through the air again, but this time a bright light shot out from his fingers and he thought he could faintly see something through the glare. He squinted his eyes to get a better look, but could only make out a shimmery image through the screen.

Danny cried out. Michael was drawn back to him and gasped when the fourteenth light come on. A huge explosion of light and sound rocked the inside of the car and a fierce wind came out of nowhere and forced him against the seat. He tried to pull himself up, to go to Danny, but the force of the wind kept pummeling him back. He screamed for the others, but they were lost in the intensity of light and images, as if a strobe light was pulsating at maximum power right in Michael's face. Now he was truly terrified, and he involuntarily threw up his hands in front of his face to protect himself.

Michael couldn't believe the driver of the limo wasn't aware of what was happening inside his cab, even with the privacy panel up. The noise itself was deafening.

"Dobber, please tell me what's happening," Michael begged. He tried to call out to the agent again, but his eyes played tricks on him. Michael stared at Dobber, but it seemed he was looking at him from an impossible distance, as if they were not sitting inside the limo at all, but in a different world. It was as if he had been transported to another time and place, a different dimension, yet he knew that couldn't possibly be true because he could feel the leather of the seat on his palms when he touched it.

The strobe light paused for a brief second, the images freezing for a mere moment, allowing Michael to see Danny and what he saw amazed him. His brother sat quietly with his hands raised to the sky, completely unaffected by the tumult he had created. And, he was smiling.

The barrage continued for another minute and during that time Michael discovered the images weren't simply random flights throughout the car. There was a pattern that actually centered on his brother, with birds circling him and flying in and out of his outstretched palms. As Danny opened and closed his fists, it seemed he beckoned more and more birds to him until finally there were so many, Michael lost sight of his brother again.

It was at that moment a huge bald eagle swooped directly into Michael's face. He shut his eyes, preparing himself for the inevitable collision. Instead, the most incredible thing happened. Instead of colliding with him, the eagle flew right through him, and Michael's head was surrounded by light. He swooned as the most glorious feeling of serenity and calm passed through him. He opened his eyes and, for a second, he saw sheer bliss. He smelled the purest of new dawn roses and heard the gurgling of water cascading over rocks from a stream at the bottom of a deep, lush valley. A feeling of tranquility and absolute acceptance filled him for a brief instant. As suddenly as it occurred, the image vanished and Michael was back in the car, straining to return to the place he had seen and felt only moments before.

He opened his eyes and became aware there weren't as many images in the car as before. In fact, he could now see his brother clearly. The racket was getting exponentially quieter. The birds were leaving. Danny's eyes were open, and he stared at the machine. As if by magic, the dials slowly turned themselves to the off position and each of the lights went out. With the disappearance of each light, the sounds, the humming, and the images of the birds slowly died out until only one light was left.

As the last light blinked out, Danny turned to Dobber, who smiled proudly at him. "You did great, Danny. Better than ever. Your mother and father will be very proud."

Michael stared at him, incredulous. "Dobber, talk to me. What just happened? What'd he just do?"

"What did he do?" he asked. "Only the most incredible thing on Earth. He turned on the fourteenth light, is what he did. Your brother's powers are almost at their fullest potential."

Danny got up and sat next to Michael, his eyes wide, seeking approval. "Did you like what I did?"

Michael was touched. Even now, after this wondrous display of his powers, his little brother was still looking to him for acceptance. He wouldn't let him down. "Danny, it was the most incredible thing I've ever seen."

Danny smiled. "Did you see the birds?"

Michael nodded, biting his lip. He wanted Danny to explain to him what he had experienced. "Danny, I have to ask you about something. While the birds were flying around the car, it was like I disappeared for moment, like one of the birds took me someplace. It was an incredible place, but I have no idea where it was. Do you know what I'm talking about?"

Danny nodded. "You saw where the birds are always looking to go. Want to know something neat? I can hear things when I go near it. And I can talk, too."

Michael was shocked. He was remembering the sound of the waterfalls and the rustling of the wind through the trees.

"There are no disabilities in the light, Michael. Everyone is the same," Dobber said. "Tell me, what exactly did you feel when you were there?"

Michael tried to express what he felt, but couldn't put it into words. "All I know is it was fantastic. A place I want to go back to."

Dobber nodded. "And that's with just a brief flicker of insight into this most wondrous of worlds. Imagine if you had the opportunity to stay even longer? Your brother is an icon of its power. He sees and feels more of this place than any other living person, and he's the truest of mediums between these two dimensions." He turned to Danny. "Danny, what did you feel this time? Was it different than the last time you were with your mother?"

Danny paused for a moment, appearing to weigh the question. "I felt the pull of the light this time. The fourteenth light made the pull much stronger and the birds trying to go there were calling out to me. I tried and tried to turn on number fifteen, but I couldn't do it. I guess I'm not strong enough yet."

"Don't be upset about that, Danny," Dobber said, patting his shoulder affectionately. "You did fine. More than fine. Your powers are growing each time you do this. Do you feel it?"

Danny smiled and nodded.

"You want to go there, I can tell."

"I love it there!" Danny exclaimed. "The birds call my name, and they talk to me there. They tell me things, and I understand them. I want to go back."

"You will soon, Danny. It truly is a wonderful place, but you must be patient and learn all you can so you can help those who can't get there on their own. What did they say to you this time?"

Danny paused again, staring at Dobber intently and then shrugged. "I don't know. Just stuff."

If Michael didn't know better, he would swear Danny was hiding something.

Dobber didn't seem to feel that way. He patted Danny's knee. "That's okay. What you discussed is private between you and those from above. You don't need to share it with me. What's important is you learn what it takes to help those who can't help themselves."

"The ones who are lost," Danny said.

"Yes. For they're the ones who truly belong there. The rest of us are just visiting until it's our time to go."

Michael listened to this entire conversation, enthralled. "Dobber, what happens when he gets to level fifteen?"

Dobber sighed and raised his hands. "To tell you the truth, Michael, we don't know, but we have an idea. Each level brings Danny and those around him to a higher plane than Earth. Your parents and I believe level fifteen will lead Danny directly to the light, if not to much more. By finally learning how to turn on that part of his power, harness his ability, it should give him the ability to transcend to this level whenever he wishes."

"But then what?" Michael asked. "What would he do there?"

Dobber shrugged. "Hopefully, when he reaches his truest potential he'll be able to tell us what's burning in the minds and souls of every person on this planet. What really happens to us when we die? This question is at the core of every major religion. Wars are fought over it. People believe in God and faith because they need to know that once they leave this world, there is something for them to go to. The truth will change everything, our beliefs in religion, our place in the universe. We may eventually all be able to unite under one true belief."

No one said anything for quite a while. There was no need.

After fifteen minutes the car stopped and pulled over to the shoulder of the highway. Michael heard someone running towards them. The door opened and it was another of the agents who had ridden on the plane with Michael.

"Dobber, we couldn't get you on the phone, and we've got news," the agent said. "We located one of Herrington's facilities. It's an island off of a small coastal town in California. And get this, we found some documents Gary had sent us discussing the huge mice issue they had when he and Maddy were in training. How they had to keep their supplies stored up high so the mice wouldn't get them. Daley thinks that's where they are."

"We're heading over there now, so follow us." The agent slammed the door and ran back to his car.

Within seconds they were speeding down the highway towards their parents.

Chapter Twenty-Two

Monday 7:00 a.m.

They had been sitting in the limo, a block from the outside of the marina, for well over an hour.

Michael was getting anxious. "What's taking them so long?"

As soon as he said it, Dobber's cell phone rang.

He answered, not taking his eyes off Danny. "Yes…okay, I understand…no. No. Okay, goodbye."

Dobber shook his head. "They've been scouring the area for almost an hour and they haven't turned up anything. I'm sorry but they don't think this is where they're keeping your parents."

Frustrated, Michael slammed his fist against the door. "So what are we going to do now?"

"You, and your brother, are going to remain here in the car where it's safe," he said. "In the meantime, I need to go and confer with Mr. Daley to decide what we need to do next."

"Are you sure they're not here?" Danny asked. "Are you positive?"

Dobber glanced at Danny curiously. "I know you're as anxious as we all are to find your parents, but the agents looked really hard and couldn't locate them. We need to figure out the next place we should concentrate our investigation. Right now they're looking at other islands or old pharmaceutical facilities and I need to discuss this with them. Don't worry, we'll find them soon." Dobber got out of the car.

"Wait a second," Michael yelled. "So, you're just going to leave us here? You can't do that. Mr. Daley said you wouldn't leave us alone again, and besides, we want to help. I can't just sit here and do nothing."

Dobber shook his head. "I'm sorry, but it's too dangerous. We can't risk the two of you walking around right now. You guys will be safer in the car until I get back. And don't worry. You won't be alone. Agent Frank is right up front. Just hit the privacy control panel and he'll answer any questions you have. I'll be back soon." He got out and shut the door. Michael heard the doors lock from the outside and threw himself back against the seat, frustrated he was being treated like a child.

This was just great. Now what were they going to do? He stared at the ceiling, wishing he could punch a hole through it and escape through there. Realizing the futility of the thought, he turned to his brother who was being extremely quiet. The sound of a motorboat sounded outside. Michael turned to Danny. "What are you doing there, Birdman?"

Danny bit his lower lip in concentration. Without Dobber seeing, he had stuck the sleeve of his jacket into the doorjamb when Dobber slammed the door and the lock hadn't fully connected.

A huge grin spread across Michael's face. "You want to get out of here as much as I do, don't you?"

Danny nodded.

"Well now, far be it for me to tell you what to do, huh?" He leaned over and tried to wiggle the doorjamb with the jacket. Taking a glance at the front panel and seeing the privacy panel still up, Michael leaned back and with his legs, kicked the door hard. It flew open and they were out.

"Well, now what?" he thought, waiting for the driver to come out and confront him. He didn't.

"Now we have to find Mommy and Daddy," Danny signed and pointed. "They're out there, you know."

Michael peered in the direction Danny pointed, staring at a large island about a quarter mile off shore. It was wooded, but a large white building peeked through the trees. While boats moved towards the island and the marina itself was thick with motorboats, no one was on the dock. In fact, it was eerily silent.

Danny pulled on Michael's arm. "Dobber wasn't telling the truth."

Michael's eyes widened. Never in all his years would he have thought he would have let a six-year-old rule his life, but his brother had proved to him he was not a regular kid. He knew things. Bad things. "Why don't you think he's telling the truth?"

"Because when I was at level fourteen I was able to talk to some of the people there. They told me to look at one of the pictures I took from the bad people's car." He removed one of the three photos from his pocket. "See? Look at this picture. The people told me this picture is the place Mommy and Daddy are being kept prisoner. This is the place the bad men took them."

Michael turned it over and saw it was dated approximately fifteen years ago. It was a picture of two men standing in front of big boat, an island in the background. Michael looked up and then back at the picture, startled to see the exact shape of the island in both photos, sans the building. Staring at the photo, Michael recognized his father. He was thinner and had a crazy looking mustache, but it was his dad. The next guy looked exactly the same as he did now, except his cheeks were covered by a thick blond beard. It was Dobber.

Michael was thunderstruck. "Oh my, God. This really is the same place, isn't it?"

"And Dobber's in the picture, too," Danny signed.

Michael considered this for a moment, biting his lip. "I know, but that doesn't mean he lied, Danny. He and Dad have known each other for a long time. Maybe he just doesn't recognize this place." He thought for a moment. "Forget it. I'm putting my money on your birds. If the FBI can't find Mom and Dad, then we will." They crept around the car quietly so as not to alert the driver.

He and Danny inched slowly up to the front of the limo. Michael risked a glance in the front seat and a glance was all he needed. Agent Frank stared blankly at a hole in the windshield, one which was exactly the same size as the one in his forehead. A dead pigeon lay on the hood of the vehicle, its neck broken.

Michael pushed his brother back against the car, his heart beating frantically. "Danny, don't look!"

"What's wrong?" Danny asked.

Michael closed his eyes. He couldn't believe that even when they were in the hands of the FBI, they weren't safe. He turned to his brother. "Danny, something really bad has happened, and I don't want you to be frightened. Someone killed Agent Frank, and I don't want you to see him."

He tried to think of who could have done this and realized it could only have been Dobber. Michael didn't want to think Dobber had lied to them. That would have been too much. For God's sake, Mr. Daley had put them into Dobber's charge. He had a horrible thought. What if Mr. Daley was against them, too? How many times had that thought crossed his mind over the past few days?

He weighed their options and there weren't many. It had to be Dobber and Daley didn't know. If Dobber was a traitor then he must have known about this place all along and led them here alone because he knew the FBI wasn't in on it. That's why no one else was around. He probably purposely lost the other agents and then diverted the car to this location. Michael shuddered when he thought of how close they had come back in the car when Danny was under the spell of the machine. Thank God, he never got to level fifteen. Then Dobber would have known the secret. He angrily slammed the car door.

Danny pulled on his arm. "Dobber killed Agent Frank, didn't he? I knew it."

Michael whirled on him. "You knew? How? From what the birds told you?"

Danny nodded. "When I got to level fourteen one of the birds told me to be careful. He told me Dobber was hiding something from us, and we had to watch out for him. After the birds told me about the picture, they told me not to try to go any higher or Dobber would see things he shouldn't, at least until he told us his secret. So, I didn't go any higher." He looked at his brother slyly. "You know, I could've gone straight to level fifteen. I'm strong enough now to do it."

"Oh, Birdman, you really are incredible," Michael said. He stared at the island. "You really think Mom and Dad are there?"

Danny nodded. "I know they are."

"Then come on," Michael said. He glanced around and when he didn't see anyone he moved quickly down the plank and started jumping into different motorboats, checking for keys. "Found one, come on, Danny." Danny jumped in and Michael, who had gone fishing with his dad on numerous occasions with their own personal motorboat, revved it up, untied the ropes from the posts, and moved out of the marina. "Danny, crouch down. I don't want anyone seeing you." Michael saw a hat on the floor of the boat and put it on his own head. "I'm going to steer us to the far side of the island, away from the main dock in front and bring us in on a shallow area so we aren't seen."

With that, they moved across the channel towards the island.

The island loomed in front of them and Michael cut the engine, letting the boat drift towards the shore. Tar balls and kelp riddled the small beach. No one was around and, as Michael stared at the tall pine and oak trees along the shore, the only sounds he heard were the shuffling of lizards and mice which hopped and skittered along the sand.

"Come on, Danny," Michael said, helping his brother into the water. He took off their shoes, dangling them from his shoulder and they waded to shore. They put their shoes back on and moved through the trees.

The island was rocky, wooded and bigger than it appeared from the shoreline. They moved past remnants of old buildings and small abandoned homes, a declaration that at one time people had lived on the island full time.

Through a dense copse of trees loomed a bright building of white marble. It was the same one they could see from the shore, glittering in the sunlight. The front windows were so dark, you couldn't see inside. As he peered around a trunk he tensed, watching Dobber walk into the building with a group of armed men and holding Danny's machine. If he had thought Dobber was still on his side, this sobered that thought in an instant.

Michael and Danny inched around the building until they were by an open garage loading dock. It was large, easily able to fit multiple trucks bringing supplies from the mainland. They moved to the inside steel door, opening it only a crack as it was exceedingly heavy, but peeking through Michael could see an empty hallway. He patted Danny and gently pushed him aside. Then, with both hands, Michael grasped the doorframe and pulled. His shoulder muscles heaved with the effort, and Michael felt another tear in the shoulder he had injured, but he didn't stop. Slowly, the door gave way, an inch at a time. Once he got the momentum going, it gave completely and opened right up. In front of them was a long passageway, brightly lit by fluorescent bulbs, which shined brightly on the white linoleum floors and traveled the entire length of a stark hallway. Michael heard voices coming from the far end of the hall and they moved cautiously in that direction.

Chapter Twenty-Three

Day 8 Monday 7:45 a.m.

A conversation echoed down the corridor from a room somewhere in the middle. Michael and Danny inched closer until they were outside.

A man screamed a litany of obscenities, and it chilled him to think he might be the one holding his parents captive. Then his stomach lurched when he heard the man speak to none other than Dobber, his parents' once trusted friend. He was so livid he had to stop himself from storming in there and attacking them both.

"Dobber, what do you mean, they're gone? Are the men searching the marina?"

"Mr. Herrington, they are, and the cameras saw the kids take one of the boats and move towards the island. They're here someplace. Don't worry, we'll find them."

"You better find them, Dobber. I won't have everyone let two children escape from me again and again. I want that boy."

Michael smiled to think he had gotten Dobber in trouble with Herrington. Good, served him right.

"Of course, Mr. Herrington. Until then, what's our next step with regards to the hostages?"

Michael clenched his fists. They were talking about his parents!

"They have fifteen minutes to cooperate with us, otherwise Gary is gone. I don't need him anymore, anyway. Then, with her husband dead and her children missing, Maddy'll have nothing. Which is just what she deserves."

A loud commotion broke out from down the hallway. Michael grabbed his brother, and they raced back down the corridor in the opposite direction. Within seconds they reached the far wall and made a quick right, out of sight. Breathing heavily, Michael peeked around the corner.

Five men stormed into the room with Herrington. There were shouts, and Michael heard chairs being overturned, before complete and utter silence ensued. He was about to walk down the hall again, but stopped when he heard Herrington. His tone was pure evil. "I should have known."

A second later there was a deafening gunshot, which reverberated up and down the hall. Herrington and his men left the room and continued down the opposite hallway on some unknown mission, but Dobber wasn't with them.

Michael grabbed Danny's hand and they snuck down the hallway. Michael glanced inside and there, on the floor against the far wall, was Dobber. He was slumped over and blood gushed from a chest wound. He glanced up with stricken eyes when he saw the boys.

"Michael, get him out of here," Dobber pleaded, his voice hoarse. "My cover's blown. I can't protect you anymore."

Michael felt no sympathy for him. "Protect us? How could you possibly have protected us? You were going to turn us in. You've been a traitor the whole time!"

"No, you're wrong," he said. "I've always been on your side. Herrington's people just found out I work for the FBI. That's why they shot me."

Michael refused to take the bait. He continued relentlessly. "So why did you desert us in the limo? Why did you take the machine to Herrington? Why did you shoot Agent Frank!"

"Oh, Michael, it's so complicated," he said, coughing up blood. "Some of those men were double agents with me, but Agent Frank was one of Herrington's people. We've infiltrated this facility and almost had it under control, but they found out. I don't know how, but they did. Please, you must get away. Go out the way you came in. I can't protect you." He went into another coughing fit. Blood spurted from his mouth and poured freely from his chest wound.

Danny moved into the room.

Michael grabbed his arm. "I don't trust him, Danny."

Dobber's body stiffened, and he stared at Danny with frightened eyes. "What is it, Danny? What's happening to me?"

"It's your time," Danny signed.

"My time?" he said dazed, his gaze wandering around the room. "Oh, yes, I guess it is." Slowly, his eyes came back into focus. "Danny, it's so much different from what I thought it would be. I'm scared."

"Don't be scared," Danny signed. "It's just level fifteen, Dobber. You're dying. You shouldn't fight it. Mommy says it makes it harder. Just let it happen or else your soul will lose the light and you'll roam the Earth."

Michael whirled on his brother. "Dobber is going to the light? Why is he going to the light?" That wasn't possible. The man was a traitor.

Danny stared at Michael solemnly. "He was good, Michael. The birds made a mistake."

Michael's jaw dropped. "They made a mistake? What do you mean?"

Danny shrugged helplessly. "I don't know. I guess they don't know everything."

Michael felt like he had been sucker-punched. The guilt ate at his stomach when he realized Dobber had gotten shot trying to protect them. He ran over to him. "Dobber, no." He was crying now, pressing frantically against Dobber's chest, trying to stop the blood from pouring out. It was no use. The wound was too deep, and Dobber was too far gone. He was no longer responding to either Michael or Danny. Instead, he focused on a spot right above Danny's head.

A beautiful white dove materialized and flew over to Dobber. Michael watched teary-eyed as Dobber's body stiffened and then slumped lifelessly against the floor.

Danny smiled at the bird. Its shimmery image drifted slowly towards the ceiling and then disappeared before their eyes.

"Did you just send him away, Danny?" Michael asked miserably.

Danny shook his head. "I didn't have to. He could find his own way. That wasn't a real bird Michael, just an illusion because there aren't any birds in this room. Dobber wasn't a bad guy. He was just hiding his identity from us so we wouldn't give him away. That was his secret."

Michael turned to his brother angrily. "But what about what you learned at level fourteen? The people there made you think Dobber was bad. He got himself killed because of us."

Danny's cast his eyes downward and started to cry. "I'm sorry. It's all my fault. I didn't understand their message."

Chagrined, Michael moved over to Danny and hugged him tight, trying hard not to look at Dobber's lifeless body. "I'm sorry. I know it's not your fault. Maybe some of those birds on level fourteen did make a mistake, but whatever advice they gave us, they knew enough to tell you about the photograph. They were trying to protect us. The fact is, if we had known the truth about Dobber earlier, there's a possibility we would have screwed up and done something to blow his cover sooner."

"I know," Danny sniffled. "But all he was trying to do was help us and now he's dead."

Michael stared at Dobber, sickened. He turned to his brother. "Danny, we can't be expected to know what the FBI, Herrington, and those from above are trying to tell us. Right now we have to just think of protecting ourselves and finding Mom and Dad. That's our number one priority." He stood. "Listen, we have to make a choice. I want to find Mom and Dad and we know they're here someplace, but my job is to protect you. That's the least I can do for Dobber—try to heed his last words. Do you want to leave? We can go back out the same way we came in."

Danny shook his head vehemently. "I want to find Mommy and Daddy."

"Me, too, but it's dangerous and I don't have any weapons. I don't know what I'd do if Herrington grabbed you."

Danny started begging. "Michael, we have to try. Mommy and Daddy are here, and we can't leave or they're going to die. I know it. Please don't make us go away."

Michael shook his head and smiled. "You're so brave, Birdman. Okay, we'll stay. We'd never be able to live with ourselves if we ran away, would we?"

Danny shook his head.

"Then, let's go." They made their way out of the room and followed Herrington's trail.

The facility was quiet, the hallways empty. Michael and Danny peeked into many of the rooms they passed, each filled to capacity with various types of scientific equipment.

They came to a set of double doors and Michael pushed them open, revealing a staircase. He heard voices echoing from above. With a quick glance at his brother, they made their way up the steps, peeking around the open double doors on the floor above. It led out to another hallway.

He followed the voices until they came to a door. As they inched up closer, Michael noticed it was open a crack and he peered inside. It was all he could do not to cry out.

Herrington was screaming at someone and grabbed a woman by the hair. Michael shuddered when he saw her black eye and the tears running down her face. It was his mother. The dress she had worn the night of the awards was covered in blood and practically in tatters. Black rage nearly blinded him. He pushed Danny back against the wall and held him there.

"Maddy, your cover's blown and Dobber's dead. I killed him myself."

Maddy gasped. "Please, I can explain."

Herrington threw his mother to the floor. "Explain? You can explain nothing. The boys are here on the island, and my men are searching for them as we speak. I found your lab, the documents, and I have the machine sitting in my office. I don't need traitors like you any longer." He turned to his guards. "Kill her."

Maddy grabbed Herrington's leg, pleading. "Please, leave my boys alone. They know nothing. I can still help you. Help you with the machine. You don't know how it works. I promise I'll tell you, just leave my boys alone."

Michael closed his eyes for a moment against the sound of his mother's begging.

Herrington pulled his leg disgustedly from her grasp and moved away from her. "As soon as we understand how Danny's powers work, which I'm sure won't take too long, I'm going to lock him up. Perfect little lab rat, don't you think? As for Michael, my data indicates he has no special powers." He stared at Maddy evilly. "I have a few new strains of viruses to try out. Think he'll agree to be my guinea pig?"

Maddy screamed, "Don't you touch him!" She stood and ran towards Herrington.

"Kill her!" he ordered, as one of the guards aimed his gun. Just as he was about to fire, Michael's father sprang from where he had been lying silently on the floor. He flew across the room and threw himself in front of Maddy.

"No!" Maddy let out a blood-curdling shriek, as the gun went off. She grabbed her husband as he fell to the floor. "Gary, oh, Gary," she screamed, over and over. She desperately tried to stop the blood from pouring out of his chest. Once she realized it was futile, she turned to Herrington with the most intense look of hatred in her eyes. "I'll kill you for this." She flew towards him. He shot her point blank in the stomach. She fell to the ground, right on top of her husband.

In less than ten seconds Michael's life was shattered, and he lost all sense. Shrieking, he flew into the room, collapsing onto his parents, and sobbing hysterically.

"Get him," Herrington ordered.

The guards grabbed Michael and forced him to his feet.

Herrington stormed over and grabbed his hair, forcing Michael to face him. "Where's Danny?"

Michael spit in his face.

Disgusted, Herrington reeled back and punched Michael in the stomach. "You're worthless, just like your parents." He turned to his guards. "Go find the kid, he won't be far away."

Michael struggled against his captors, trying to find his breath. "Leave my brother alone," he wheezed. "He can't help you."

"We'll see about that." Herrington glanced at his guards again. "Now go. Get me Danny."

"He's right here, Mr. Herrington," another guard said quietly. He held Danny's lifeless body in his arms. "He's dead, Mr. Herrington."

Herrington's eyes bulged in incomprehension. "What do you mean he's dead? Was he shot?"

The guard shook his head. "No, sir. There's no blood or anything. He was just lying in the hallway, outside this door. I checked his pulse. There's nothing. He's dead, sir."

Michael started screaming, fighting his captors. "You murderers. You killed my brother and my parents." With renewed strength he pulled free and hurled himself at Herrington.

Herrington took out a knife from his arm sheath, but before Michael reached him, Michael's body convulsed. His back became rigid and his head arched back, gagging sounds coming from his throat.

"What's the matter with him?" Herrington asked, dropping the knife in surprise.

"I don't know," the guard answered, confused.

Michael's eyes rolled back in his head, before his entire body went limp. He collapsed in the guard's arms.

The guard laid him on the ground and took his pulse. He glanced up at his boss, stunned. "He's dead too, Mr. Herrington. I don't understand."

Herrington screamed out a host of obscenities, grabbed a chair, and threw it across the room. He stormed over to Michael and seized his arm, trying to jerk him to his feet. Michael's body remained limp. Disgusted, Herrington threw him onto his mother. Then he stormed over to Danny, picked him up, and threw him on top of his father.

Michael watched through half-closed eyes, paralyzed and unable to move. He was drifting, like he was falling into a deep sleep. In the distance, Herrington ranted about poison and antidotes, how the Andersons would rather have their children dead than have him learn about Danny's powers. He commanded the rest of the guards to locate the FBI spies who had infiltrated the facility and described the penalty they'd incur if he found anyone else who had slipped through his grasp.

Just as Michael was about to fade out completely, he heard Herrington bark one final order to another guard who just came into the room.

"Bob, it's about time you got here. Wrap up the bodies. I'm taking them to the mainland. Let's try to salvage something from this."

As the last vestiges of consciousness left him, he heard the reply. "Of course, Mr. Herrington."

It was the voice of Mr. Daley.

Chapter Twenty-Four

In the Light

Michael blinked. Where was he? He drifted though a rainbow. Slowly, he extended his hand into the prism of colors. A beam of light extended from each of his fingers, each reflecting a different color of the spectrum. He gazed around him, noticing how he floated through the sky, drifting up higher and higher, circling towards a beautiful beam of brilliant white light. The illumination was so radiant he thought he might have to look away, or his eyes would get burned. Instead, he found he could stare directly at it and see right through its glare. In fact, the more he stared, the more he thought he saw someone within the glow waving at him.

"C'mon, Michael!"

It was Danny.

"I'm coming, Danny," he cried out ecstatically, soaring towards his brother. "You can hear me?"

"Yes, I can. Now, come on! We've been waiting for you—and do I have something to show you." He disappeared from view.

"I'm coming, wait up," Michael called back, as he flew directly into the light. Suddenly, the image changed. He was no longer in the clouds and alone. He was no longer flying, but standing in a beautiful valley surrounded on all sides by green mountains. It was the same place he had visited in the limousine when the bird flew right through him, though now the feeling and experience was magnified a thousand-fold.

He gazed to his right at a brook lined with rose bushes and hundreds of different kinds of flowers. The perfume the blossoms gave off was intoxicating and made him feel slightly drunk. As he laughed out loud in unexplained joy he felt around him the presence of multitudes of birds and souls. Once he realized they were there he couldn't help but see them by the thousands, and he thought he should feel claustrophobic. Instead, it was the most natural feeling in the world.

"Danny, where are we?" He wanted to ask more questions, but stopped. That's when he saw them.

"Mom! Dad!"

Both his parents emerged, unhurt, from behind a grove of trees, Danny in the rear. Michael sprinted towards them, and though he felt himself running, it was more like gliding. What would have taken him thirty seconds to do down below, he could do here in five. Michael bounded into his mom's and dad's arms as they descended on him with hugs and kisses.

"Oh, my boy," his mother cried, squeezing him so hard she took his breath away. "My sweet boy."

He turned to his father. "Dad."

Gary cried, slapping him on the back and then grabbed him into a huge bear hug. "Oh, Michael. I couldn't have trusted Danny with anyone more than I trusted him with you. I am so very proud of you."

"Hey, look everyone!" Danny called out, pointing up to the sky. "There's a whole new group coming in."

They all gasped as thousands of pure white doves suddenly filled the sky. The light from the sun bounced off each of the doves and formed a rainbow which showered a glittering cascade of colors onto each of them until they were no longer bathed in sunlight but in brilliant, sparkly hues of red, yellow, and blue.

"Danny, what is it?" Michael laughed, delightedly as rainbow colored snowflakes seemed to fall around him.

"Just the new souls coming in," Danny said. "It's beautiful, isn't it? They're going on higher."

"What's higher than here, Danny?" Michael asked. "This must be Heaven because I can hear you. Did we make it to level fifteen?" Abruptly he stopped smiling and he stared at his brother, panicked. "Oh, my God, this means I'm dead, doesn't it? We all are, aren't we?" He gazed at his family and felt overwhelming grief.

His mother patted his arm. "Michael, Danny explained some of it to us while we were waiting for you. We're not dead, yet. As soon as Herrington shot your father and me, Danny took himself straight to level fifteen and brought us with him. I don't understand how he did it, but he had us bypass the transgression phase where we would remain in our bird bodies until we took ourselves into the light. It seems we never went into them at all and just came straight here. He wanted it to look like we died so Herrington would leave us alone, but we're actually still alive, though barely. Our souls can be brought back and as soon as it's safe Danny will lead us back into our bodies. Did I explain it right, Danny?"

Danny nodded and smiled. He glanced down and watched the ground intensely. Michael followed his gaze, but all he could see was the ground covered with green grass and tiny yellow wildflowers. "What is it, Danny?"

"I can see Mr. Daley," he explained. "He's so sad. He doesn't know what to do."

"Bob is down there?" Gary asked.

Danny nodded. "Herrington still believes he's one of them, and he thinks all of us are dead."

"Wait, but what about me?" Michael asked. "I didn't get shot, but I remember something happening to me. Like I had a seizure or something. How did I get here?"

Danny gave him a solemn expression. "I brought you here."

Michael immediately understood the implications. "So, you killed me somehow, didn't you? How did you learn how to do that?"

Danny laughed and shook his head. "I didn't kill you. I just borrowed your soul for a little while. Then I took yours and mine and left our bodies back in the lab room and came here. This way Herrington would think we died. Later, after it's safe, we can go back and get away."

Michael turned to his mother. "Mom, how can he do this?"

Maddy seemed at a loss. "I had no idea the depth of Danny's powers. This wonderful place is as much a mystery to me as it is to you and your father. But taking us here is not the only change I've noticed in him. It's not just that he can hear and speak now, but also how he speaks. It's as if he's all grown-up."

Danny turned to her, grasping her hand. "Mommy, I'm older here. I can understand more. I think it's these souls talking to me. It's all because of the light."

Michael was confused. "Wait a second. I still don't fully understand. Isn't this the light? Isn't this Heaven?" He let his eyes explore the paradise surrounding him.

"This is level fifteen, but this isn't Heaven," Danny said. "Heaven's up there." He pointed to the sky above them.

Michael stared amazed as he tilted his head straight up. He was incredulous that he hadn't noticed this phenomenon before now. Above him was what appeared to be a humongous ruby colored crystal sparkling gloriously in every conceivable direction. Around this crystal were hundreds of pinpoints of light, each pulsing and glowing and casting piercing streaks of white illumination which reflected back to the crystal and bounced off from it. Each ray that extended from the crystal resembled a fire burst which shot out all around it. "What is that, Danny? It looks like a gem."

"It's the ultimate place," Danny whispered. "It just looks like a gem to us, but it's really just the power of all light. If we flew up there and went into it, I think we'd disappear. That's what I hear from the souls from above. Once you go there, it's not like Earth with trees and flowers and birds. It's like nothing we've ever experienced. Just one vast place where everyone converges into each other. You can create your own dream world there and even though there are millions and millions of souls, you're still an individual in a group of many."

"But if this isn't Heaven, then what is this place?" Michael asked.

"It's a resting place for those whose bodies are still alive on Earth," he said. "It's a place to go to when your soul can't decide if it's time to leave or not. Once you make the decision you can either go back to Earth or go up higher. We can stay here until we decide what to do."

"Son, are we to go up? Is that our fate?" Gary asked, staring longingly at the sky.

Michael knew what his father was feeling. There was a pull on his very being to go further.

Danny shook his head. "No, Daddy. I know how it feels, but it's not our time yet. Not for any of us. We can't go, and I can't send you. I don't have the strength."

Gary smiled. "I don't really want to go, son. I just feel it pulling on me. It's like a gentle tug, caressing my arm."

Maddy spoke up. "Danny, honey, when can we go back down?"

Danny nodded. "Soon, but one of us has to go and let Mr. Daley know to get us out of there. Mommy and Daddy, you need to get out of the lab and to people who can help you before I put you back into your bodies. You're both really hurt, and you'll be too weak to get out yourselves. The bleeding has stopped for the moment, but if you move before you have help it will start again. Then you really will go to the light."

"Danny, it's okay," Gary said. "I'll be the one to go. I don't want to risk any one of you getting into Herrington's hands again. Not after all you've been through. I can do this with Bob. Daley and I go way back. He'll find a way to get us out."

"Gary, don't be ridiculous," Maddy said. "Didn't you hear what Danny just said? You were shot at point blank range. I saw it. How are you going to walk around with a bullet in your chest and not bleed to death? If Danny says you'll die, then you have to listen to him." She took Michael's arm. "It's got to be Michael, doesn't it?"

Danny nodded. "Both you and Daddy can't go and neither can I. I have to stay here and make sure you don't wake up on your own. Michael's the only one who can go back and help Mr. Daley get us out."

"Danny, how will you know when it's safe?" Michael asked. "How will you know when it's the right time?"

"Don't worry, I'll know," he said, waving his hands around. "Everyone here will help me." Flitting in and out of the air were hundreds of transparent birds. "And, Michael, I'll be able to see you, too. As soon as I'm sure Mommy and Daddy are safe, I'll bring us back. I promise." He turned and suddenly hugged Michael fiercely. "You are the best big brother in the world."

Michael's eyes began to tear. "Oh, boy, Birdman. You have a way of saying just the right thing. Okay, send me back before I chicken out. This place is so beautiful I don't want to leave." He stepped away and smiled at each of them.

Danny closed his eyes and suddenly hundreds of birds materialized in the air. One of them made a dive, straight at Michael. Again he found himself shutting his eyes, thinking the bird was going to crash into him. Instead, it went inside him and he felt his body changing.

"We love you, Michael," he heard his family calling out, as he plummeted downward, fast, back to Earth at heart-wrenching speeds. Within seconds the calm feeling he had felt with his brother was replaced by the hard tiled floor and the feel of his mother's limp, soft hand under his arm. Slowly, he opened his eyes and saw Daley slumped next to them in a chair, his face in his hands.

"Mr. Daley?" he called out softly. No matter how softly he said it, it still wouldn't have made it any easier for Mr. Daley. Startled, he jumped up and cried out.

"Michael?" he asked, confused. He rushed over to him.

Michael smiled, and slowly sat up. "Yeah, it's me. I'm okay."

Michael could see the relief in Mr. Daley's eyes. "Oh, thank God. I thought we'd lost you, too." He looked sadly over at Michael's family lying next to him.

"I'm sorry, Michael. I'm so sorry about your family. There was nothing I could do." He leaned close to Danny and gently stroked his cheek.

"Yes, there is, Mr. Daley," he said, pointing at his parents. "You can help me, and help them."

"Michael, they're beyond help. What we need to do is get you out of here right now. Come on!" He tried to pull Michael to his feet and out of the room.

"Mr. Daley, wait. My parents aren't dead."

Daley stared at him. "Michael," he began carefully, "I examined them myself. I'm sorry, but there is nothing else we can do for them."

Instead of crying, which is what anyone would have expected Michael to do, he laughed. As Daley stared at him stupefied Michael said, "Boy, do I have something to tell you that'll blow your mind."

Chapter Twenty-Five

"Michael, keep your head down," Daley whispered, while he ushered him through the hallway, pushing the remaining members of the Anderson family in a storage cart. "And stop fidgeting."

"I'm having trouble with the pants." Two sizes too big, he hitched up the stolen lab uniform used by the scientists during quarantine procedures. He paused to pull the safety cap lower over his brow.

There was a commotion from the end of the hall and three men appeared.

"Okay, here we go," Daley murmured. "Two of Herrington's men, Johnson and Gallagher and one of our own, a double-agent named Sean. Just keep your cool, follow my lead, and don't say a word."

The three men approached. "So, you've got corpse duty, Daley?" Johnson laughed. "What's the matter? You get on Herrington's bad side so he finally pulled you from the cushy school job?"

"Oh, leave him alone, Johnson," Sean said. "It could just as easily be you doing this. And will be soon if Herrington finds out you've been dipping into his stash."

Johnson straightened up. "No sense of humor, any of you. Fine, get rid of them, though I hate to see Maddy go. She was fine to look at in the lab, I'll tell you that." He winked at them. "As for the kid? I never thought there was anything special about him anyway." He slapped Danny on the back of his head.

Michael wanted to grab him and break his neck.

Daley shrugged. "I just take orders, Johnson." He began to pull the cart down the hallway as Michael pushed.

Suddenly Gallagher, who had been quiet, spoke up and sauntered towards Michael. "Wait! I don't remember Herrington hiring any children. What, this a new genius interning with us? Come here, kid." Though Michael moved quickly, Gallagher deftly made a grab for his cap and yanked it off his head.

Gallagher stepped back, shocked. "It's the Anderson kid." He turned to Daley, his expression stunned. "You're a traitor, Daley? After all these years?" He drew his gun.

"Gallagher, I'm not a spy," Daley said, buying time. "You're making a mistake. This isn't the boy you think it is."

Out of the corner of his eye Michael saw Agent Sean quietly take a long knife out from inside his shirt.

Gallagher yelled, advancing towards Michael. "Liar. The boy must be taken out." He trained his gun at Michael.

"Michael, run," Daley ordered.

Michael immediately took off down the hallway, when suddenly a massive ripping noise tore through the building and it felt like the entire facility lifted and slammed to the floor. He fell to the ground with a violent crash, rolling over repeatedly as sirens shrieked through the building.

Terrified and not understanding immediately what was happening, Michael tried to stand, but the building was shaking so badly he fell to the floor again. The sprinklers came on dousing him and as he tried to rise someone slammed him to the floor, their knees pinned to his chest and a pair of hands squeezed his neck so hard he couldn't breathe. As his world came in and out of focus a gunshot rang out, once, twice and as he was about to black out from lack of oxygen, the hands released.

Seconds later, Daley was by his side, Sean next to him. "Come on, Michael, we have to get out of here while we can. We're having an earthquake."

Michael nodded, coughing, and crawled across the sopping wet floor to the cart, which held his family. It was shaking and slamming into the wall.

The three of them pushed the cart down the hall when the shaking ceased.

"Is it over?" Michael asked. He had never been in an earthquake before. Just then, the ground started shaking again. He felt like the world was falling apart.

Daley grimaced. "Not yet. Now we get the aftershocks." They swung the cart towards the elevator.

"We're going in there?" Michael asked, appalled. "In an earthquake?"

Daley nodded. "Only way to get your folks down. Don't worry. This facility is supposedly earthquake-proof. Herrington made it so nothing will stop those elevators. The guy is scared of them and made this his number one priority for the building so he'd never get locked in." They pulled up to them, and he slammed his hand to the button as he slipped, nearly falling.

Shouts echoed from the staircase on the far end of the hall and Michael saw armed guards trying to get down the hall. They were thrown into the walls, falling down, but kept getting back up. One aimed and fired, the bullet hitting the wall next to Michael.

The elevator opened. "Get in," yelled Daley, shoving the cart inside. The three of them piled in and Daley hit the button, the elevator doors slamming shut as another round of bullets riddled the door.

As the elevator descended, a roar like a giant train rumbling shook the elevator and Michael fell to the floor. The elevator vibrated so drastically he was sure the entire structure was going to crumble into a million pieces around him.

And then silence.

Michael glanced around him. Daley and Sean picked themselves shakily up off the floor, holding onto the cart, which miraculously was still holding Michael's family.

The elevator had stopped moving.

Daley hit the buttons, but nothing happened. He picked up the phone, but it was dead. Placing his ear to the elevator door, he listened, furrowing his brow. "I think I hear something." He tried to manually open the door but stopped when the sudden flapping and cawing of thousands of birds screeched through the walls of the elevator. Terrified, Michael threw himself back against the wall, holding his hands to his ears to drown out the excruciating noise of hundreds of bird's talons scraping against the metal frame of the elevator.

Human screams met their ears. The elevator vibrated and shook again, throwing them to the ground. The cart collided with Michael, and he bumped his head. For a split second it seemed as if the world had stopped, but then it was eerily silent yet again.

Daley again put his ear to the door, but this time all was quiet. After a quick glance at Michael, he and Sean shoved their fingers in the middle of the elevator doors and started to pry them apart. Once it was open a bit, Sean grabbed his gun, covering Daley until they had the door wide open. Miraculously, they were on ground level.

"Stay behind us, Michael," Daley ordered as they moved into the downstairs lobby. As they wheeled the cart into the room, they stared, shocked, into the dead faces of Herrington's guards littering the floor. Blood was everywhere and the carnage had been vicious. Long, piercing cuts ran the length of their bodies and their faces appeared to have been picked apart by someone, or something, with very sharp claws.

"Were they attacked by a pack of wild animals?" Agent Sean asked, amazed.

Daley glanced at Michael knowingly. "Birds, Sean. They were attacked by birds."

Michael pointed to a dead bird on the floor. In fact, there was a dead bird next to each and every one of the guards. "These guys aren't going anywhere."

He turned to Daley. "It was Danny who did this. He sent the birds to help us. My job was to get my parents out of the lab room and only then would he be able to help us." He faced the ceiling. "Thanks, Danny." He could swear he felt his brother smiling at him.

They wheeled the cart outside the room and through a large swinging door, which led to the outside of the facility. They were met with an awesome spectacle.

The once silent island was now filled with FBI agents and police officers swarming around, handcuffing Herrington's people and escorting them to boats to take them to the mainland. Michael glared as he watched Herrington being dragged out from a side building. He had a long gash running down his cheek and his left eye bled freely. He was screaming hysterically at a woman being taken from another building on a hospital gurney and shuttled onto a boat.

Three of Daley's men raced to them.

"We got any extra paramedics here?" Daley asked.

One of the agents nodded, speaking into his walkie-talkie. Within seconds paramedics were racing towards them.

Michael spoke. "I know it looks like everyone in my family has been killed, but they're not, trust me."

The paramedics glanced at the Andersons and stalled for just a moment until Daley barked at them. "Treat these people as if they're still alive."

Immediately, Maddy, Gary, and Danny were placed on gurneys of their own and moved quickly towards the harbor port. From Michael's vantage point, he could see the entire marina, loaded with police boats and military personnel.

Daley turned to one of the guards. "What exactly went on here? How did you get them into custody?"

"We were hoping you could explain some of it for us," the agent said. "We were hiding along the shoreline, waiting for a sign, any sign you had gotten to Maddy and Gary when the earthquake occurred. It was all we could do to keep our positions, when the most incredible thing happened. As if a giant thundercloud had erupted, thousands upon thousands of birds flew from the mainland straight into the facility. Windows had shattered from the earthquake, and the birds tore into every available opening to get inside. They went into storm drains, air vents, sewers. Any place there could have possibly been an opening. And I'm talking thousands, Daley. The sky was pitch black. We heard screaming coming from the building and then Herrington's men charged out, literally throwing themselves into our hands. Birds were everywhere, attacking them and as soon as Herrington's people got near us the birds simply disappeared. I mean disappeared, right in front of our eyes. It was the most incredible thing I've ever seen."

Daley nodded at Michael. "Yes, incredible, isn't it?"

Michael just grinned and moved with Daley to the docks.

They glanced up at the commotion coming from one of the boats where Michael's parents had been placed. The trauma paramedics were racing around frantically and Michael's heart swelled when he saw his mother raise her hand and place it on her forehead. The boat started and immediately moved away, speeding towards the mainland.

Michael jumped onto another boat with Daley and they followed his parents and Danny. As the wind whipped his face, he turned to Daley. "I think it's finally over, isn't it?"

"Yes it is, kid. It's over."

As the boat left the island, Michael glanced back to the pier. A beautiful group of white doves sat on top of a group of pillars, quietly watching as they sped away.

Epilogue

Early August, three months later

It was a perfect summer afternoon. Daley was hosting a picnic at his summer home in the Pennsylvanian mountains. Easily a hundred people were on the lawn, FBI members and their families, munching on hot dogs and burgers, playing volleyball, and swimming in the lake.

Michael waded out of the water, carrying Danny on his back and they jogged over to their parents.

Gary and Maddy were both lying on a blanket on the beach, basking in the rays.

"Did you see me do a back flip off the dock, Mommy?" Danny signed excitedly. Michael had just taught him how to do this, and he couldn't get enough of it.

"I saw you, sweetheart," she signed. "Just be careful, okay?"

"Oh, Mom," Michael said. "What're you worried about? You know he can't get hurt. Don't you see the twenty birds that gently push him away from the side every time he gets too close? Everyone should have twenty guardian angel's surrounding them."

Both Gary and Maddy had required extensive surgery after their ordeal and after weeks of recuperation, they were released from the hospital.

The government had cleared Michael of all murder charges and the Andersons of any espionage charges and rented the family a house in a new town where they wouldn't be as easily recognized. By the second week of July, both Gary and Maddy were working in the lab part-time, but now their research was public. That is, the research on light therapy for seniors.

Maddy started laughing. "Twenty guardian angels, huh? Well, I still believe it's a good thing we're the only ones who know what they really are. I don't think the world is ready to know the truth yet."

Gary placed a comforting hand on his wife's shoulder. "But they will be soon, hon."

They turned to watch Danny. He had moved to sit with a lone seagull at the edge of the water.

"Send him on his way, Danny," Michael whispered. He watched his brother close his eyes. The seagull's body slowly rose and flew into the sky.

The three of them smiled, staring at the image which soared higher and higher until it finally disappeared.

"Look at him, Mom. Isn't he wonderful?" Michael watched his brother laughing and waving at the soul drifting up into the clouds.

Flying to the light.

About the Author

Elyse Salpeter loves "mixing the real with the fantastic" in her novels. She is the author of several other works, including a YA dark fantasy series, THE WORLD OF KAROV and THE RUBY AMULET. She is also the author of a new adult thriller series. Book #1 is called, THE HUNT FOR XANADU.

When she isn't writing, she's eating crazy foods in her gastronaut club, chasing after her twins and crazy ferret, and all summer long you'll see her working to get weeds out of her garden. By the end of the summer, they've usually won the battle.

Excerpt of Book #2 in the FLYING series

FLYING TO THE FIRE

"One sees up, and the other sees down..."

Prologue

Seven and a half years ago, in a seaside villa off the coast of California...

The sound of the monitor whispered and hissed as the man slipped into the bedroom. The startled nurse rose from her chair and left. She was careful not to look him in the eye.

When he was sure he was alone, the man turned to the patient in the hospital bed and moved to her side. Now that he was closer, he could hear the sharp intake of her breath and see the way her chest rose and fell with each ragged breath. This wasn't supposed to happen to her. Not to his Marta.

She had once been so beautiful. Thick blond hair had brushed past her shoulders in soft curls and she had a regal, aquiline profile. She had reminded him of a queen who was supposed to stand by his side and rule the world with him. Now most of her hair had fallen out and her features were pinched with pain.

Marta slowly opened her eyes, those blue gems that most people thought were cold, but to him were fountains of pure, unadulterated beauty. "Samuel," she whispered.

He placed his hand on her forehead. Her skin was so brittle, his simple touch bruised her, and she winced. He quickly pulled his hand away. "I'm not going to let you go, Marta. That's unacceptable to me and I won't tolerate it."

She gave him a pitiful expression. "You have no choice. It's a wonder I've lasted this long. We both know that."

Samuel tried not to think about the accident. How one of his lab technicians had carelessly mixed up a quarantined experimental disease with a simple compound and brought it into the general lab where his wife had been working.

The moment the imbecile had uncorked it, Marta realized from the smell what had been released. She immediately put the facility on lockdown, even while the disease began to attack her vital organs. Emergency protocols were activated and the staff evacuated behind sealed doors. Only Samuel chose to break protocol and equipped with the finest bio-hazard suit, had gone in to get Marta and bring her out, leaving his lab tech to die a torturous death on the floor of the lab room.

His team of scientists and doctors worked feverishly to wipe out the effects of the disease on her system. Within days, the infection had run its course, but the damage to her body had been done. Her organs were permanently weakened and there was nothing any of them could do about it.

Or was there?

"Marta, I won't let death separate us."

"You speak in riddles, Samuel. Since when is death not the end?"

"I have a way to bring you back to me and it's based on the Anderson's theories. Let me tell you my idea." He leaned towards his wife's ear and whispered what he planned to do. Over and over again, day in and day out, so that when she finally left this earth, the knowledge would remain in her subconscious. For he believed that death was not the final resting place and that her very soul and consciousness would still be alive. Somewhere.

He had to find the younger Anderson boy. The child knew about the afterlife and Herrington was determined to extract every single piece of information he could from him. His men were already on the hunt and it would only be a matter of time before he would learn what he needed to bring his wife back to this world.

#

But that never happened. A week later he was caught by the FBI, the boy had gotten away, Marta died in a secret facility out east, and he was incarcerated for a lifetime sentence in prison. His plans had failed.

Or had they?

Chapter One

Seven and a half years later, in upstate New York…

It was the best thirteenth birthday present ever. The new bike was awesome. Much more awesome than the old one with the beat up handlebars, chipped green paint, and ripped nylon seat. Danny pumped the pedals harder, feeling the gravel crunch under his feet. Michael had told him the sound resembled paper crumpling.

He'd have to take his word for it.

He'd had the bike for nearly six months, and he still marveled at how it performed, as if it had been designed especially for him. Gripping the handlebars, he jumped the curve and veered the bike onto the dirt path and into the woods. His calves burned as he raced through the fallen leaves. Wayward branches scratched at his cheeks, but he didn't care. He loved the feel of zooming through the forest and the freedom he felt when he was going so fast it was hard to breathe. Mostly, he loved the way it made him forget about things, like the nightmares he'd been having nearly every night--the one with the dark black twister that tried to suck the life out of him.

He shook his head to clear it and pumped harder, streaking through the path. He was glad his dad had put off-road tires on this one. He could feel the difference.

It was unseasonably chilly for late October, and his breath steamed in the air in front of him like a plume of smoke. Danny veered around a turn in the bend and was about to rush out of the woods and through Magnolia Fields when the air rippled in front of him and a huge black apparition like a tumultuous storm cloud appeared in his path.

With a yelp, he gripped the brakes on the handlebars too fast and flipped forwards headlong into and through malignant mist, falling hard on the ground. His head crashed into a dead log. Thank God he had his helmet on. For a moment, stars covered his vision. The smell of decayed animals and rotted food overcame him, and he gagged violently. Sitting up, he felt a bitter coldness seep deep into his body. He gripped himself tight as the darkness closed in like a fog. He began to shiver and his fingers turned blue. Danny fell back to the ground and tried to catch his breath.

Little chunks flew out of the mass and hit his face. He realized they were bits and pieces of bugs and worms, some squirming onto his cheeks and others falling onto his arms and body. He started to fight, punching at the presence, but it was as if he were smacking against air. The pressure of this manifestation continued to get stronger and it physically pushed him to the earth as it forced its power against him. He could feel its energy and the way it was charging. Charging? That was impossible.

Danny's chest tightened as the mass pressed against it, crushing him bit by bit. He opened his mouth wide and screamed, hoping someone would hear him. With one last desperate attempt, he pulled into himself, felt the familiar electric push in his head and sent his thoughts upwards and out of his body. As he was about to black out from lack of air, he stared at the sky and that's when he finally saw them. They had heard his call and soared towards him. With a relief so profound, he knew he wasn't alone, and that they would help him. In a fury of wings, a throng of birds descended and threw themselves into the black mass.

The mass released Danny to fight the birds and with the pressure gone, Danny turned over and wheezed and coughed violently. He tried to rise, but a wind picked up and threw him back to the ground again. The black mass spun and twisted itself into a spinning, whirling funnel. Danny was sucked into it as if he were in the path of a tornado. It dragged and whipped him through the dirt, his body flipping and turning in the brush until he was thrown against a small pine tree. He grabbed desperately at the low lying branches, ignoring the tears in his skin and the strain in his arms as the mass fought the birds, who again and again were flung out of the funnel, only to keep thrusting themselves back in.

A hummingbird was hurled at his feet. Its neck was broken and Danny tried to reach out to save it, but it was sucked back into the void of blackness, only to get thrown back to the ground repeatedly. Just before Danny thought he couldn't hold on any longer, the charges in the air changed and the mass retracted into itself and sucked back into the earth. In a heap of wings, the multitude of birds fell to the ground in thuds so hard, he could feel it in his chest.

With a sob, Danny crawled to them, touching each, one by one. Backs and wings broken, their necks twisted, he finally found one alive, laying within a mass of crushed insects. He cradled the quivering cardinal in his palms. Leaning down and whispering to it, the bird opened one of its black eyes, and stilled. A white light shot out of Danny's fingers and a shadow raced from his hands to the sky, disappearing into the clouds.

Danny turned to the other birds and, sniffling, gathered them together. He glanced into the woods, seeing shadows floating and bobbing in the trees. He shook his head sadly, knowing there was nothing he could do to help any of them. Placing the fallen birds in a pile, he covered them with a makeshift grave of dirt and leaves and said a little prayer. Looking at the woods, tears in his eyes, he nodded to the forlorn shapes and watched as they disappeared within the woods.

With an effort, Danny pulled up his battered, shaking body and grabbed his bike. He walked it out of the woods and into the field. Halfway through, he turned and saw the black hulking mass had returned, now teetering at the edge of the trees. It appeared to be watching him and it was pulsating. Danny could feel the hairs on his arms stand up and could feel the energy of the beast as it was charging. How was it doing that? But then the mass collapsed into itself, oozing and spreading out like black oil, and with a ripple, sucked itself again into the ground.

Danny stood there trembling. He felt something wet tickle his cheek. He grabbed it with his hand, glanced at it and threw it to the ground.

It was a bloody, wiggling brown slug. He wiped his face with his shirt and saw a coat of slime covering his sleeve. With a shudder, he jumped onto his bike and hurried home.

The thing from his dream was no longer imaginary. The black mass was here and it was real.

And there was nothing he could do about it.

If you'd like to learn more about Elyse and her writing, please visit her at the following sites:

www.elysesalpeter.com

www.facebook.com/elysesalpeterauthor

www.twitter.com/elysesalpeter

www.elysesalpeter.wordpress.com

Printed in Great Britain
by Amazon.co.uk, Ltd.,
Marston Gate.